'You're offering to make coffee?'

'Is there something wrong with the idea of a man making coffee?'

Ouch. Angel had just been sexist and he'd called her on it. Fairly. 'I guess not.'

'Don't make assumptions,' he said softly. 'Especially if you're basing them on what the press says about me.'

Was he telling her that he *wasn't* the playboy the press suggested he was? Or was he playing games? Brandon Stone flustered her. Big-time. And she couldn't quite work out why. Was it just because he was so good-looking? Or did she see a tiny hint of vulnerability in his grey eyes, showing her that there was more to him than just the cocky, confident racing champion? Or was that all just wishful thinking and he really *was* a shallow playboy?

What she *did* know was that he was her business rival. One who wanted to buy her out. Part of her thought she shouldn't even be talking to him.

Dear Reader,

This book started off when my husband and I visited an Open Garden day at a local stately home and rather fell in love with some of the vintage cars on display. I'd also been discussing *Romeo and Juliet* with my daughter. And then I thought… What would keep two families at loggerheads in modern times? And what if the son of one family and the daughter of the other fell in love with each other? And what if the heroine had been *really* wrapped in cotton wool? (I needed a reason for her to be wrapped in cotton wool: I borrowed that from my own deafness, which is from precisely the same cause as Angel's.)

I also wanted to throw a few things on their head. Brandon thinks he has everything planned out and can be ruthless—but what he *doesn't* expect is to find himself falling in love. And once things start to go badly wrong how is he going to save the day?

I hope you enjoy reading Brandon and Angel's story as much as I enjoyed writing it!

With love,

Kate Hardy

HIS SHY CINDERELLA

BY
KATE HARDY

This is a work of fiction. Names, characters, places, locations and
incidents are purely fictional and bear no relationship to any real
life individuals, living or dead, or to any actual places, business
establishments, locations, events or incidents. Any resemblance is
entirely coincidental.

First Published in Great Britain 2017
By Mills & Boon, an imprint of HarperCollins*Publishers*
1 London Bridge Street, London, SE1 9GF

© 2017 Pamela Brooks

ISBN: 978-0-263-06892-4

Our policy is to use papers that are natural, renewable and recyclable
products and made from wood grown in sustainable forests. The logging
and manufacturing processes conform to the legal environmental
regulations of the country of origin.

Printed and bound in Great Britain
by CPI Antony Rowe, Chippenham, Wiltshire

Kate Hardy has always loved books, and could read before she went to school. She discovered Mills & Boon books when she was twelve and decided *this* was what she wanted to do. When she isn't writing Kate enjoys reading, cinema, ballroom dancing and the gym. You can contact her via her website: katehardy.com.

For Gerard,
who answered a lot of very weird questions
about motor racing with a great deal of patience
(but I am still not going to a Grand Prix with you!). xxx

CHAPTER ONE

ANGEL FLICKED THROUGH the pile of mail on her desk.

Bills, bills, circulars and—just for a change—bills. Bills she really hoped she could pay without temporarily borrowing from the account she'd earmarked for paying the company's half-yearly tax liability.

And there was still no sign of the large envelope with an American postmark she'd been waiting for, containing the contract for supplying the new McKenzie Frost to feature in the next instalment of *Spyline*, a high-profile action movie series. Triffid Studios hadn't emailed to her it instead, either, because Angel had already checked her inbox and the spam box. Twice.

Maybe she'd send a polite enquiring email to their legal department tomorrow. There was a fine line between being enthusiastic about the project and coming across as desperate and needy.

Even though right now Angel felt desperate and needy. She couldn't let McKenzie's go under. Not on her watch. How could she live with herself if she lost the company her grandfather had started seventy years ago? The contract with Triffid would make all the difference. Seeing the McKenzie Frost in the film would remind people of just how wonderful McKenzie's cars were: hand-made, stylish, classic, and with full attention to every detail. And they were bang up to date: she intended to produce the Frost in an electric edition, too. Then their waiting list would be full again, with everyone wanting their own specially customised Frost, and she wouldn't have to lay anyone off at the factory.

Though she couldn't even talk about the deal yet. Not until she'd actually signed the contract—which she couldn't do until her lawyer had checked it over, and her lawyer couldn't do that until the contract actually arrived...

But there was no point in brooding over something she couldn't change. She'd just have to get on with things as best as she could, and hope that she didn't have to come up with plan B. And she didn't want to burden her parents with her worries. She knew they were enjoying their retirement, and the last thing she wanted was to drag them back from the extended vacation they'd been planning for years.

She'd grin and bear it, and if necessary she'd tell a white lie or two.

She went through the post, dealing with each piece as she opened it, and paused at the last envelope: cream vellum, with a handwritten address. Most people nowadays used computer-printed address labels, or if they did have to write something they'd simply grab the nearest ballpoint pen. This bold, flamboyant script looked as if it had been written with a proper fountain pen. Disappointingly, the letter itself was typewritten, but the signature at the bottom was in the same flamboyant handwriting as the envelope.

And her jaw dropped as she read the letter.

It was an offer to buy the company.

Selling up would be one way to solve McKenzie's financial problems. But selling McKenzie's to Brandon Stone? He seriously thought she would even consider it?

She knew the family history well enough. Her grandfather had set up in business with his best friend just after the Second World War, building quality cars that everyone could afford. Except then they'd both fallen in love with the same woman. Esther had chosen Jimmy McKenzie; in response, Barnaby Stone had dissolved their business partnership and left with all the equipment to go and start up another business, this time based on making factory-built cars. Jimmy McKenzie had started over, too, making his hand-built cars customisable—just as McKenzie's still built their cars today.

On the eve of the wedding, Barnaby Stone had come back and asked Esther to run away with him. She'd said no.

Since then, the two families had never spoken again.

Until now.

If you could call a letter speaking.

Angel could see it from Brandon's point of view. Buying McKenzie's would salve his sense of family honour because then, although the grandfather had lost the girl, the grandson had won the business. It would also be the end of everything McKenzie's did, because Stone's would definitely get rid of their hand-made and customised process. She knew that Stone's racing cars were all factory built, using robots and the newest technology; it was the total opposite of the hand-craftsmanship and personal experience at McKenzie's.

She'd heard on the grapevine that Stone's wanted to branch out into making roadsters, which would put them in direct competition with McKenzie's: and what better way to get rid of your competitor than to buy them out? No doubt he'd keep the name—McKenzie's was known for high quality, so the brand was definitely worth something. She'd overheard her parents discussing it during the last recession, when Larry Stone had offered to buy McKenzie's. According to her father, Barnaby Stone had been a ruthless businessman, and his sons and grandsons came from the same mould. She knew Max McKenzie was a good judge of character, so it was obvious that Brandon would asset-strip the business and make all her staff redundant.

No way.

She wouldn't sell her family business to Brandon Stone, not even if she was utterly desperate and he was the last person on earth.

And what did he really know about business, anyway? Driving race cars, yes: he'd won a few championships in his career, and had narrowly missed becoming the world champion a couple of times. But being good at driving a racing car wasn't the same as being good at running a business that made racing cars. As far as she knew, dating supermodels and quaffing magnums of champagne weren't requirements for running a successful business either. She was pretty sure that he was just the figurehead and someone else did the actual running of Stone's.

Regardless, she wasn't selling. Not to him.

She flicked into her email program. In his letter, Brandon Stone had said he looked forward to hearing from her at her earliest convenience. So she'd give him his answer right now.

Dear Mr Stone

No way is the McKenzie's logo going on the front of your factory-made identikit cars. I wouldn't sell my family business to you if you were the last person on earth. My grandfather would be turning in his grave even at the thought of it.

Then she took a deep breath and deleted the paragraph. Much as she'd like to send the email as it was, it sounded like a challenge. She wasn't looking for a fight; she was simply looking to shut down his attempts at buying her out.

What was it that all the experts said about saying no?
Keep it short. No apologies, no explanations—just no.

Dear Mr Stone
    Thank you for your letter. My company is not for sale.
Yours sincerely
Angel McKenzie

She couldn't make it much clearer than that.

When his computer pinged, Brandon flicked into his email
program. Angel McKenzie was giving him an answer already? Good.

Then he read the email.

It was short, polite and definite.

And she was living in cloud cuckoo land.

She might not want to sell the business, but McKenzie's
was definitely going under. He'd seen their published accounts for the last four years, and the balance sheet looked
grimmer every year. The recession had bitten hard in their
corner of the market. The way things were going, she
couldn't afford not to sell the company.

Maybe he'd taken the wrong approach, writing to her.
Maybe he should try shock tactics instead and be the first
Stone to speak to a McKenzie for almost seven decades.

And, if he could talk her into selling the company to
him, then finally he'd prove he was worthy of heading up
Stone's. To his father, to his uncle, and to everyone else
who thought that Brandon Stone was just an empty-headed
playboy who was only bothered about driving fast cars.
To those who were just waiting for the golden boy to fail.

He glanced at the photograph of his older brother on his
desk. And maybe, if he could pull off the deal, it would
be the one thing to help assuage the guilt he'd spent three

years failing to get rid of. The knowledge that it should've been him in that car, the day of the race, not Sam. That if he hadn't gone skiing the week before the race and recklessly taken a diamond run, falling and breaking a rib in the process, he would've been fit to drive. Meaning that Sam wouldn't have been his backup driver, so he wouldn't have been in the crash; and Sam's baby daughter would've grown up knowing her father as more than just a photograph.

Brandon wasn't sure he'd ever be able to forgive himself for that.

But doing well by Stone's was one way to atone for what he'd done. He'd worked hard and learned fast, and the company was going from strength to strength. But it still wasn't enough to assuage the guilt.

'I'm sorry, Sammy,' he said quietly. 'I'm sorry I was such an immature, selfish brat. And I really wish you were still here.' For so many reasons. Sure, Brandon would still have been working in the family business by this point in his career—but Sam would've been at the helm of the company, where he belonged. Nobody would've doubted Sam's managerial abilities. And their uncle Eric wouldn't have been scrutinising Sam's every move, waiting for an opportunity to criticise.

He shook himself. Eric was just disappointed because he thought that he should be heading up the business. Brandon needed to find him a different role, one that would make him happy and feel that he had a say in things. If Brandon could bring McKenzie's into the fold, then maybe Eric could take charge there.

Getting Angel McKenzie to sell to him was definitely his priority now. Whatever the personal cost.

He rang her office to set up a meeting.

'I'm afraid Ms McKenzie's diary is full for the next

month,' the voice on the other end of the line informed him, with the clear implication that it would be 'full' for the month after, too, and the month after that.

Like hell it was.

Clearly Angel had anticipated his next move, and had briefed her PA to refuse to book any meetings with him.

'Maybe you could email her instead,' the PA suggested sweetly.

Any email would no doubt find its way straight into her trash box. 'I'll do that. Thank you,' Brandon said. Though he had no intention of sending an email. He'd try something else entirely. When he'd replaced the receiver, he went to talk to his own PA. 'Gina, I need everything you can find about Angel McKenzie, please,' he said. 'Her CV, what she likes doing, who she dates.'

'If you're interested in her, sweetie, shouldn't you be looking up that sort of thing for yourself?' Gina asked.

Oh, the joys of inheriting a PA who'd known you since you were a baby and was best friends with your mum, Brandon thought. 'I'm not interested in dating her,' he said. 'This is work. Angel McKenzie.' He emphasised the surname, in case she'd just blocked it out.

Gina winced. 'Ah. *Those* McKenzies.'

'I already know the business data,' he said. 'Now I need to know the personal stuff.'

'This sounds as if it's going to end in tears,' Gina warned.

'It's not. It's about knowing who you're doing business with and being prepared. And I'd prefer you not to mention any of this to Mum, Dad or Eric, please. OK?'

'Yes, Mr Bond. I'll keep it top secret,' Gina drawled.

Brandon groaned. 'Bond's PAs used to sigh with longing, flutter their eyelashes and do exactly what he asked.'

'Bond didn't have a PA. He flirted with everyone else's

PAs. And you can't flirt with someone who changed your nappy,' Gina retorted.

Brandon knew when he was beaten. 'I'll make the coffee. Skinny latte with half a spoonful of sweetener, right?'

She grinned. 'That's my boy.'

'You're supposed to respect your boss,' he grumbled, only half teasing.

'I do respect you, sweetie. But I also think you're about to do something stupid. And your mum—'

'Would never forgive you for letting me go right ahead,' Brandon finished. He'd heard that line from her quite a few times over the years. The worst thing was that she was usually right.

He made the coffee, then buried himself in paperwork.

Gina came in an hour later. 'One dossier, as requested,' she said, and put the buff-coloured folder on his desk.

She'd also printed a label for the folder, with the words *Top Sekrit!* typed in red ink and in a font that resembled a toddler's scrawled handwriting.

'You've made your point,' he said. She thought he was behaving like a three-year-old.

'Good. I hope you're listening.'

Given that Gina was one of the few people in the company who'd actually batted his corner when he'd first taken over from his father, he couldn't be angry with her. He knew she had his best interests at heart.

'There aren't going to be any tears at the end of this,' he said gently. 'I promise.'

'Good. Because I worry about you almost as much as your mum does.'

'I know. And I appreciate it.' He reached over to squeeze her hand, hoping he wasn't about to get the lecture regarding it being time he stopped playing the field and settled down. Because that didn't figure in his plans, either. How could he ever settle down and have a family, knowing he'd taken that opportunity away from his brother? He didn't deserve that kind of future. Which meant his focus was strictly on the business. 'Thanks, Gina.'

'I've emailed it to you as well,' she said. 'Don't do anything stupid.'

'I won't.'

The top of the file contained a photograph. Angel McKenzie looked like every other generic businesswoman, dressed in a well-cut dark suit teamed with a plain white shirt buttoned up to the neck, and her dark hair cut in a neat bob.

But her eyes were arresting.

Violet blue.

Brandon shook himself. An irrelevant detail. He wasn't intending to date her.

Her CV was impressive. A first-class degree in engineering from a top university, followed by an MA in automotive design from another top institution. And she hadn't gone in straight at the top of her family business, unlike himself: it looked as if she'd done a stint in every single department before becoming her father's second-in-command, and then Max McKenzie had stepped aside two years ago to let her take charge. Again, impressive: it meant she knew her business inside out.

But there was nothing in the dossier about her personal life. He had the distinct impression that she put the business first and spent all her time on it. Given the state of those balance sheets, he would've done the same.

But there was one small thing that he could use. Angel McKenzie went to the gym every morning before work. Even more helpfully, the gym she used belonged to the leisure club of a hotel near to her factory. All he had to do was book a room at the hotel, and he could use the leisure club and then accidentally-on-purpose bump into her.

Once they were face to face, she'd have to talk to him.

And it would all be done and dusted within a week.

At seven the next morning, Brandon walked into the leisure club's reception area and paused at the window. The badge on the woman's neat black polo shirt identified her as *Lorraine, Senior Trainer.*

'Good morning,' he said with a smile. 'I wonder if you can help me.'

She smiled back. 'Of course, sir. Are you a guest at the hotel?'

'I am.' He showed her his room key.

'And you'd like to use the facilities?'

'Sort of,' he said. 'I'm meeting Angel McKenzie here.'

'It's Thursday, so she'll be in the pool,' Lorraine told him. 'Would you like a towel?'

'Yes, please.' And he was glad he'd thought to bring swimming trunks as well as a T-shirt and sweatpants.

She handed him a thick cream-coloured towel. 'I just need you to sign in here, please.' She gestured to the book on the windowsill with its neatly ruled columns: name, room number, time in, time out. 'The changing rooms are through there on the left,' she said, indicating the door. 'The lockers take a pound coin, which will be returned to you when you open the locker. As a guest, you also have use of the sauna, steam room and spa pool. Just let us know if you need anything.' She gave him another smile.

'Thanks.' He signed in, went to change into his swimming gear, and followed the instructions on the wall to shower before using the pool.

The pool room itself was a little warm for his liking. Nobody was sitting in the spa pool, but there were three people using the small swimming pool: a middle-aged man and woman who were clearly there together, and a woman who was swimming length after length in a neat front crawl.

Angel McKenzie.

Brandon slid into the water in the lane next to hers and swam half a dozen lengths, enjoying the feel of slicing through the water.

Then he changed his course just enough that he accidentally bumped into her, knocking her very slightly off balance so she was forced to stand up in the pool.

He, too, halted and stood up. 'I'm so sorry.'

She looked at him. The first thing he noticed was how vivid her eyes were; the photograph had barely done her justice.

The second thing he noticed was that she was wearing earplugs, so she wouldn't have heard his apology.

'Sorry,' he said again, exaggerating the movement of his mouth.

She shrugged. 'It's OK.'

Clearly she planned to go straight back to swimming. Which wasn't what he wanted. 'No, it's not. Can I buy you a coffee?'

She took out one of the earplugs. 'I'm afraid I missed what you said.'

'Can I buy you a coffee to apologise?'

'There's no need.' She was starting to smile, but Brandon saw the exact moment that she recognised him, when her smile disappeared and those amazing violet eyes narrowed. 'Did you bump into me on purpose?'

He might as well be honest with her. 'Yes.'

'Why? And what are you doing here anyway?'

'I wanted to talk to you.'

'There's nothing to say.'

He rather thought there was. 'Hear me out?'

'We really have nothing to talk about, Mr Stone,' she repeated.

'I think we do, and your PA won't book a meeting with me.'

'So you stalked me?'

Put like that, it sounded bad. He spread his hands. 'Short of pitching up on your doorstep and refusing to budge, how else was I going to get you to speak to me other than by interrupting your morning workout?'

'My company isn't for sale. That isn't going to change.'

'That's not what I want to talk about.'

She frowned. 'Then why do you want to talk to me?'

'Have breakfast with me, and I'll tell you.'

She shook her head. 'I don't have time.'

'Lunch, then. Or dinner. Or breakfast tomorrow morning.' Brandon didn't usually have to work this hard with women, and it unsettled him slightly.

She folded her arms. 'You're persistent.'

'Persistence is a business asset,' he said. 'Have breakfast with me, Ms McKenzie. You have to eat before work, surely?'

'I…'

'Let's just have breakfast and a chat.' He summoned up his most charming smile. 'No strings.'

She said nothing while she thought about it; Brandon, sure that she was going to refuse, was planning his next argument to convince her when she said, 'All right. Breakfast and a chat. No strings.'

That was the first hurdle over. Good. He could work with this. 'Thank you. See you in the restaurant in—what, half an hour?'

'Fifteen minutes,' she corrected, and hauled herself out of the pool.

Brandon did the same, then showered and changed into his business suit and was sitting at a table in the hotel restaurant exactly fourteen minutes later.

One minute after that, Angel walked in, wearing a business suit, and he was glad that he'd second-guessed her and worn formal clothing rather than jeans. Though he also noticed that her hair was still wet and pulled back in a ponytail, her shoes were flat and she wasn't wearing any make-up. The women in his life would never have shown up for anything without perfect hair, high heels and full make-up; then again, they would also have made him wait for two hours while they finished getting ready. Angel McKenzie clearly valued time over her personal appearance, and he found that refreshing.

The other thing he noticed was that she was wearing a hearing aid in her left ear.

That hadn't been in his dossier. He was surprised that Gina had missed it, but it felt too awkward and intrusive to ask Angel about it.

Then she knocked him the tiniest bit off kilter by being the one to bring it up.

'Do you mind if we swap places? It's a bit noisy in here and it's easier for me to lip-read you if your face is in the light.'

'No problem,' he said, standing up immediately. 'And I'll ask if we can move tables to a quieter one.'

She gestured to the floor. 'It's wooden floor, so it's going to be noisy wherever we sit. Carpet dampens speech as well as footsteps.'

And there was a group of businessmen nearby; they were laughing heartily enough to drown out a conversation on the other side of the room. 'Or we could change the venue to my room, which really will be quieter,' Brandon said, 'but I don't want you to think I'm hitting on you.'

Though in other circumstances, he thought, I probably would, because she has the most amazing eyes.

He was shocked to realise how much he was attracted to Angel McKenzie. She was meant to be his business rival, from a family that was his own family's sworn enemy. He wasn't supposed to be attracted to her. Particularly as she was about six inches shorter and way less glamorous than the women he usually dated. She really wasn't his type.

'The restaurant's fine,' she said, and changed places with him. 'So what did you want to talk about? If it's your offer to buy McKenzie's, then it's going to be rather a short and pointless conversation, because the company isn't for sale.'

Before he could answer, the waitress came over. 'May I take your order?'

'Thank you.' Angel smiled at the waitress and ordered coffee, granola, fruit and yoghurt.

Brandon hadn't been expecting that smile, either.

It lit up her face, turning her from average to pretty; in all the photographs he'd seen, Angel had been serious and unsmiling.

And how weird was it that he wanted to be the one to make her smile like that?

Worse than that, focusing on her mouth had made him wonder what it would be like to kiss her. How crazy was that? He was supposed to be talking to her about business, not fantasising about her. She wasn't even his type.

He shook himself and glanced quickly through the menu.

'Sir?' the waitress asked.

'Coffee, please, and eggs Florentine on wholemeal toast—but without the hollandaise sauce, please.'

'Of course, sir.'

'I would've had you pegged as a full English man,' Angel said when the waitress had gone.

'Load up on fatty food and junk, and you're going to feel like a dog's breakfast by the end of a race,' he said with a grimace. 'Food's fuel. If you want to work effectively, you eat effectively. Lean protein, complex carbs, plenty of fruit and veg, and no added sugar.'

She inclined her head. 'Fair point.'

He needed to get this back on the rails. 'So. As I was saying, this discussion isn't about buying the company.'

She waited to let him explain more.

So that was her tactic in business. Say little and let the other party talk themselves into a hole. OK. He'd draw her out. 'I wanted to talk about research and development.'

She frowned. 'What about it?'

'I'm looking for someone to head up my R and D department.' He paused. 'I was considering headhunting you.'

She blinked. 'Yesterday you wanted to buy my company.'

He still did.

'And today you're offering me a job?'

'Yes.'

She looked wary. 'Why?'

'I heard you're a good designer. A first-class degree in engineering, followed by an MA in automotive design.'

'So you *have* been stalking me.'

'Doing research prior to headhunting you,' he corrected. 'You're a difficult woman to pin down, Ms McKenzie.' And he noticed that she still hadn't suggested that he used her first name. She was clearly keeping as many barriers between them as possible.

'Thank you for the job offer, Mr Stone,' she said. 'I'm flattered. But I rather like my current job.' She waited a beat to ram the point home. 'Running the company my grandfather started.'

'Together with my grandfather,' he pointed out.

'Who then dissolved the partnership and took all the equipment with him. McKenzie's has absolutely nothing to do with Barnaby Stone.'

'Not right now.' He held her gaze. 'But it could do.'

'I'm not selling to you, Mr Stone,' she said wearily. 'And I'm not working for you, either. So can you please just give up and stop wasting your time and mine?'

He applauded her loyalty to her family, but this was business and it was time for a reality check. 'I've seen your accounts for the last four years.'

She shrugged, seeming unbothered. 'They're on public record. As are yours.'

'And every year you're struggling more. You need an investor,' Brandon said.

Angel had been here before. The last man who'd wanted to invest in McKenzie's had assumed that it would give him rights over her as well. She'd put him very straight about that, and in response he'd withdrawn the offer.

No way would she let herself get in that situation again. She wasn't for sale, and neither was her business. 'I don't think so.'

'Hand-built cars are a luxury item. Yours are under-priced.'

'The idea was, and still is, to make hand-built custom-isable cars that anyone can afford,' she said. 'We have a waiting list.'

'Not a very long one.'

That was true; and it was worrying that he knew that. Did that mean she had a mole in the company—someone who might even scupper the deal with Triffid by talking about the McKenzie Frost too soon? No. Of course not. That was sheer paranoia. She'd known most of the staff since she was a small child, and had interviewed the newer members of staff herself. People didn't tend to leave McKenzie's unless they retired. And she trusted everyone on her team. 'Have you been spying on me?'

The waitress, who'd just arrived with their food and coffee, clearly overheard Angel's comment, because she looked a bit nervous and disappeared quickly.

'I think we just made our waitress feel a bit awkward,' Brandon said.

'You mean *you* did,' she said. 'Because you're the one who's been spying.'

'Making a very common-sense deduction, actually,' he countered. 'If you had a long waiting list, your balance sheet would look a lot healthier than it does.'

She knew that was true. 'So if we don't have a great balance sheet, why do you want to buy...?' She broke off. 'Hold on. You said you want a designer to head up your research and development team. Which means the rumours are true—Stone's really is looking at moving into the production of road cars.'

He said nothing and his expression was completely inscrutable, but she knew she was right.

So his plan was obvious: to buy McKenzie's, knocking out his closest competitor, and then use her to make his family's name in a different area.

No way.

She stared at him. His dark blond hair was just a little too long, making him look more like a rock star than a businessman; clearly it was a hangover from his days as the racing world's equivalent of a rock star. And he was obviously used to charming his way through life; he knew just how good-looking he was, and used that full-wattage smile and sensual grey eyes to make every female within a radius of a hundred metres feel as if her heart had just done a somersault. He was clearly well aware that men wanted to be him—a former star racing driver—and women wanted to be with him.

Well, he'd find out that she was immune to his charm. Yes, Brandon Stone was very easy on the eye; but she wasn't going to let any ridiculous attraction she felt towards him get in the way of her business. His family had been her family's rivals for seventy years. That wasn't about to change.

'So basically you want to buy McKenzie's so you can put our badge on the front of your roadsters?' She grimaced. 'That's tantamount to misleading the public—using a brand known for its handmade production and attention to detail to sell cars made in a factory.'

'Cars made using the latest technology to streamline the process,' he corrected. 'We still pay very close attention to detail.'

'It's not the same as a customer being able to meet and shake the hands of the actual people who built their car. McKenzie's has a unique selling point.'

'McKenzie's is in danger of going under.'

'That's not happening on my watch,' she said. 'And I'm not selling to you. To anyone,' she corrected herself swiftly.

But he picked up on her mistake. 'You're not selling to me because I'm a Stone.'

'Would you sell your company to me?' she countered.

'If my balance sheet was as bad as yours, you were going to keep on all my staff, and my family name was still going to be in the market place, then yes, I'd consider it—depending on the deal you were offering.'

'But that's the point. You won't keep my staff,' she said. 'You'll move production to your factory to take advantage of economies of scale. My staff might not want to move, for all kinds of reasons—their children might be in the middle of a crucial year at school, or they might have elderly parents they want to keep an eye on.' Her own parents were still both middle-aged and healthy, but she wouldn't want to move miles away from them in case that changed. If they needed her, she'd want to be there.

'Your staff would still have a job. I can guarantee that all their jobs will be safe when you sell to me.'

'Firstly, I'm not selling, however often you ask me. Secondly, they already have a job. With me.' She folded her arms. 'Whatever you think, McKenzie's isn't going under.'

'We could work together,' he said. 'It would be a win for both companies. Between us we could negotiate better discounts from our suppliers. You'd still be in charge of research and development.'

The thing she loved most. Instead of worrying about balance sheets and sales and PR, she could spend her days working on designing cars.

It was tempting.

But, even if they ignored the bad blood between their families, it couldn't work. Their management styles were too far apart. McKenzie's had always considered their teams to be part of the family, whereas Stone's was ruthless. Between them they had two completely opposing cultures—and there was no middle ground.

'I don't think so. And there's nothing more to say,' she said. 'Thank you for breakfast.' Even though she hadn't eaten her granola and had only drunk a couple of sips of coffee, she couldn't face any more. 'Goodbye, Mr Stone.' She gave him a tight smile, pushed her chair back and left.

CHAPTER TWO

'MISS MCKENZIE? THANK YOU for coming in.'

James Saunders gave her a very professional smile which did nothing to ease Angel's fears. When your bank asked you to come in to the branch for a meeting, it didn't usually mean good news. She'd been hoping all the way here that it was just a courtesy meeting for him to introduce himself as their new account manager, but she had a nasty feeling that it was nothing of the kind.

'My pleasure, Mr Saunders.' She gave him an equally professional smile. 'I'm assuming that today is simply to touch base, as you've just taken over from Miss Lennox?'

'I'm afraid it's a little more than that. May I offer you some coffee?'

Funny how that sounded more like, 'You're going to need a stiff gin.'

'Thanks, but I'm fine,' she said. 'So how can I help?'

'I've been going through your published accounts,' James said.

Uh-oh. She'd heard that from someone else, very recently. And that hadn't been a good meeting, either.

'I need to be frank with you, Miss McKenzie. We're really not happy with the way things are going. We're not sure you're going to be able to pay back your overdraft.'

'I can reassure you that I have a deal in the pipeline,'

she said. 'Obviously I'm telling you this in strictest business confidence, because you're my bank manager, but Triffid Studios is sending me a contract because they want to use our new design in their next *Spyline* film. Once the film comes out and people see the car, our waiting list will be full for at least the next year. We'll have to expand to meet demand.'

'And you've signed this contract?'

'I'm still waiting for them to send it. The film industry seems to drag its heels a bit where paperwork's concerned,' she admitted. 'But we've built the prototype, tweaked it and they're happy with it, so it's really just a formality.' She just wished they'd hurry up with the paperwork.

'I'd be much happier if I could see that signed contract,' James said.

So would she.

'Because,' he continued, 'I'm afraid I can't extend your overdraft any more.'

'You're calling it all back in? Right now?' Angel went cold. She had no idea where she'd get the money to pay back the overdraft. Even if she could negotiate a breathing space before it had to be paid back, and put her house on the market so it was priced to sell, she still wouldn't make that much money once she'd cleared the mortgage. Nowhere near enough to prop up McKenzie's. And, unlike her father in the last recession, she didn't have a valuable private car collection to sell.

So how else could she raise the money?

'I'll give you a month to get that contract signed,' James said. 'And then I'm afraid I'll have to call the majority of the overdraft in. In these times, banks have to be seen to lend responsibly.'

And businesses like hers that were going through temporary difficulties—despite being good clients for decades—ended up as the scapegoats. 'I see. Well, thank you for your frankness, Mr Saunders.'

'I'm sorry I can't give you better news.'

To his credit, he did look a little bit sorry. Or maybe that was how bank managers were trained nowadays, Angel thought. Though he didn't look quite old enough to manage a bank.

'I'll keep you posted on the contract development,' she said.

Her next stop was at her lawyer's, to see if they could get in contact with Triffid's lawyers and persuade them to firm up a date by when they'd have the contract.

She brooded all the way back to the factory. There had to be a way out of this. The last thing she wanted to do was worry her father or burden him with her problems. He'd trusted her to run the company, and she wasn't going to let him down.

If her parents rang in the next couple of days she'd either miss the call deliberately and blame it on her deafness—she'd been in the shower and hadn't heard the phone ring—or she'd distract her father by talking car design. It was the way she dealt with the shyness that had dogged her since childhood: switching the conversation to cars, engines or business, where she was confident in her abilities, meant she didn't have to worry about the personal stuff.

But she was really worried about this.

If the bank called in their loan before the contract was signed...

She'd just have to be more persuasive. She could put a presentation together quickly enough, with sales projections, based on the new Frost. Though she had a nasty feeling that only the signed contract would be enough to satisfy James Saunders.

The more she thought about it, the more she wondered

if she should've taken up Brandon Stone's offer after all. He'd said that every job at McKenzie's would be safe. He'd implied that they'd keep the McKenzie name on the road cars. He'd even offered her a job, heading up his research and development team, though it wasn't a part of the offer she could bring herself accept. Selling to him was probably the best thing she could do for everyone else.

But how could she live with herself if she threw away seventy years of her family's history and sold out to the company started by her grandfather's ex-best friend?

There had to be another way, beyond selling the company to Brandon Stone.

Plus there was something else she needed to address. Cambridge was a reasonably small city; if anyone had seen her with Brandon the other day and realised who he was, rumours could start circulating. The last thing she wanted was for her team to be unsettled. She needed everyone to pull together.

When she got back to the office, she called a team meeting on the factory floor. Everyone looked anxious, and she knew why. 'First of all,' she said, 'I want to reassure everyone that it's business as usual. Things are a bit slow, right now, but once that new contract's signed and the PR starts, it's going to pick up and the bank will be happy again.'

'Do you want us to go on short time?' Ravi, one of the engineers, asked.

It would be another solution, but Angel didn't think it was fair for her staff to bear the brunt of the company's problems. 'No. We'll manage,' she said firmly. 'The other thing is that Stone's has offered to buy us out.'

There was a general gasp. Ernie, the oldest member of her team, stood up. 'It might not be my place to say this, but I hope you said no. I worked for your grandfather. No way could I work for a Stone. They don't do things like we do.'

'I heard their staff's all on zero-hours contracts,' someone else said. 'I can't take that risk. I've got a mortgage and kids.'

'I can't comment on how they run their business,' Angel said, 'but I'm not selling. McKenzie's will continue to do things the way we always do things. The only change is that we'll be producing a new model, and I know I can trust you to keep everything under wraps.'

'What can we do to help?' Jane, one of the leather cutters, asked.

She smiled. 'Just keep doing what you do. Make our cars the best they can be—and leave the worrying to me. I just wanted you all to know what was going on and hear the truth from me. If anyone hears any rumours to the contrary, they're probably not true, so come and talk to me rather than panic, OK?'

'If things are tight,' Ernie said, 'you could always use our pension fund to plug the gap.'

'That's a nice offer,' she said, 'but using that money for anything except your pensions would get me slung straight into jail. And I'm not asking any of you to take any kind of risk.'

'I've got savings,' Jane said.

'Me, too,' Ravi said. 'We could invest in the company.'

It warmed Angel that her team trusted her that much. 'It's not going to come to that, but thank you for offering. It's good to know that my team believes in me. Well, you're not just my team. You're *family*.'

'Your grandad would be proud of you, lass,' Ernie said. 'Your dad, too. You're a McKenzie through and through.'

Tears pricked her eyelids. 'Thank you. All of you.' She

swallowed hard. 'So is anyone worried about anything else?'

Everyone shook their heads.

'OK, You know where I am if you think of anything later. And thank you all for being so supportive.'

Though after she'd left the team she found it hard to concentrate on her work. She just kept coming back to Brandon Stone and his offer to buy her out.

What really bothered her was that she couldn't get the man himself out of her head. The way he'd looked standing up in the swimming pool, with the water barely reaching his ribs: his shoulders had been broad and his chest and biceps firm. He'd looked just as good in the restaurant, clothed in a formal suit, shirt and tie. Those grey eyes had seemed to see everything. And that beautiful mouth...

Oh, for pity's sake.

She didn't do relationships. Her parents had pretty much wrapped her up in cotton wool after her deafness had been diagnosed, and as a result she'd been too shy to join in with parties when she'd gone to university. Once she'd finished her studies, her focus had been on working in the family business.

But when Brandon Stone had accidentally-on-purpose bumped into her in the pool, her skin had actually tingled where his touched hers. And, even though she was pretty sure that he turned that megawatt smile on anyone with an X chromosome, she had to admit that she was attracted to him—to the last man she should date.

Was he really the playboy she suspected he was?

She knew he had a dossier on her, so she had no compunction about looking up details about him.

He'd started heading up the family firm three years ago. Something about the date jogged a memory; she checked on a news archive site, and there it was. *Sam Stone killed in championship race.*

Brandon hadn't raced professionally since the crash. There had been no announcements about his retirement in the press; then again, there probably hadn't needed to be. Sam's death had clearly affected his younger brother badly. And the rest of his family, too, because Brandon's father had had a heart attack a couple of weeks after Sam's death—no doubt brought on by the stress of losing his oldest child. Poor man.

Angel continued to flick through the articles brought up by the search engine. Eric Stone—Brandon's uncle—had sideswiped him a few times in the press. Then again, Brandon had walked into the top job with no real experience; Eric probably thought he was the one who should be running Stone's and was making the point to anyone who'd listen.

Angel felt a twinge of sympathy for Brandon. Everyone at McKenzie's had supported her when she'd taken over from her father. Brandon had barely had time to settle in before his father had been taken ill and he'd taken over the reins, and it wouldn't be surprising if a few people resented him for it. She'd had the chance to get to know the business thoroughly before she'd taken over, whereas he'd had to hit the ground running. Despite what she'd thought earlier about his background not really qualifying him for the job, he'd done well in running the company, using the same concentration and focus on the business that he'd used to win races in his professional driving days. From the look of their published accounts, Stone's was going from strength to strength. They certainly had enough money to buy her out.

The rest of the newspaper stories she found made her wince. Even allowing for press exaggeration, Brandon

Stone seemed to be pictured with a different girl every couple of weeks. Most of them were supermodels and high-profile actresses, and none of the relationships seemed to last for more than three or four dates. His personal life was a complete disaster zone. He really wasn't the kind of guy she should even consider dating. She should be sensible about this and stop thinking about him as anything else other than a business rival.

Brandon scrubbed his hair in the shower on Sunday morning after his run, hoping to scrub some common sense back into his head.

This was ridiculous.

Why couldn't he stop thinking about Angel McKenzie and her violet eyes—and the smile that had made him practically want to sit up and beg? It had been three days since he'd met her, and he still kept wondering about her.

It threw him, because he'd never reacted to anyone like this before. Angel was nothing like the kind of women he normally dated: she was quiet and serious, and she probably didn't even own a pair of high heels. He wasn't even sure if she owned lipstick. Though he also had the feeling that, if they could put aside the family rivalry, he'd have a better conversation with her than he usually had with his girlfriends. She wouldn't glaze over if he talked about cars and engineering.

Oh, for pity's sake. Why was he even thinking like this? He didn't want to date anyone seriously. He really wasn't looking to settle down. Seeing the way that Maria, his sister-in-law, had fallen apart after Sam's death had cured him of ever wanting to get involved seriously with anyone; even though he didn't race now, he still didn't want to put anyone in Maria's position.

But he just couldn't get Angel McKenzie out of his head.

Or the crazy idea of dating her...

And then he smiled as he dried himself. Maybe that was the answer. If he dated her, it would get her out of his system; plus he'd be able to charm her into doing what he wanted and she'd sell the business to him. It was a win-win scenario.

So how was he going to ask her out?

Sending her a bouquet of red roses would be way too obvious. Too flashy. Too corny. Besides, did she even like flowers? Some women hated cut flowers, preferring to see them grow rather than withering in a vase. None of that information was in his dossier.

He could ring her PA and talk her into setting up a meeting, though he was pretty sure that Angel had given her strict instructions to do nothing of the kind.

Or he could try a slightly riskier option. He was pretty sure that Angel McKenzie spent all her energies on her business; so there was a very good chance that she'd work through her lunch break and eat a sandwich at her desk.

If he supplied the sandwich, she couldn't really refuse a lunch meeting with him on Monday, could she?

The more he thought about it all day, the more he liked the idea.

Gina's dossier didn't tell him whether Angel was vegetarian, hated fish or had any kind of food allergies. So at the supermarket on Monday morning he erred on the side of caution and bought good bread, good cheese, heritage tomatoes, a couple of deli salads and olives.

Though he had to be realistic: Angel could still say no and close the door in his face, so he needed a plan B to make sure she said yes. And there was one obvious thing. Something that, in her shoes, he wouldn't be able to resist.

He flicked the switch to trigger his car's voice-control audio system, connected it to his phone and called Gina as he drove home. 'I'm not going to be in the office today,' he said, 'and I won't be able to answer my phone, so can you text me if there's anything I need to deal with?'

'You're taking a day's holiday?' She sounded surprised: fair enough. He didn't take many days off, and he normally gave her a reasonable amount of notice.

'This is work,' he said. Of sorts.

'And it involves a girl,' Gina said dryly.

Yes, but not quite how she thought. And he could do without the lecture. 'I'll check in with you later,' he said.

Back at his house, he collected a couple of sharp knives, cutlery, glasses and plates from the kitchen, dug out a bottle of sparkling water, put the lot into a picnic basket and then headed out to his garage. He backed one of his cars into the driveway and took a photograph of it, then put the picnic basket in the back. If Angel refused to have lunch with him or even talk to him, he was pretty sure that the photograph would change her mind.

Angel's PA gave Brandon a rueful smile. 'I'm afraid you don't have an appointment, Mr Stone, and Ms McKenzie's diary is fully booked.'

Brandon glanced at the nameplate on her desk. 'If I didn't already have a fabulous PA who also happens to be my mother's best friend,' he said, 'I'd definitely think about poaching you, Stephanie, because I really admire your loyalty to Ms McKenzie.'

Stephanie went pink. 'Oh.'

'And, because I think you keep an eye on her,' he said, 'I'm pretty sure you're the one who actually makes her take a break at lunchtime, even if it's just five minutes for a sandwich at her desk.'

'Well—yes,' Stephanie admitted.

'So today I brought the sandwich instead of you having to do it,' he said, gesturing to the picnic basket he was carrying.

'I really can't—' she began.

'Stephie, is there a prob—?' Angel asked, walking out of her office. Then she stopped as she saw Brandon. 'Oh. You.'

'Yes. Me,' he agreed with a broad smile.

'What do you want?'

'I brought us some lunch.' He focused on charming her PA. 'Stephanie, if you'd like to join us, you're very welcome.'

'I, um…' Stephanie went even pinker.

'Don't try to use my PA as a pawn,' Angel said grimly. 'And I don't have time for lunch.'

'The same as your diary's allegedly fully booked, but there's nobody actually sitting in your office right now having a meeting with you?'

She frowned. 'You really are persistent, aren't you?'

'We've already discussed that. Persistence is a business asset.'

'Wasn't it Einstein who said the definition of insanity was doing the same thing over and over again and expecting different results?' she asked coolly.

'That's been attributed to quite a few other people, from ancient Chinese proverbs to Rita Mae Brown,' he said, enjoying himself. Sparring with someone with a mind like Angel McKenzie's was fun. 'Actually, I'm not doing the same thing over and over again. This is lunch, not breakfast.'

If Brandon had driven to Cambridgeshire from his family's factory near Oxford, that would've taken him at least a couple of hours if the traffic was good, Angel thought. He'd made an effort. Maybe she should make a little effort back. If she talked to him, maybe she might get him to understand that she was serious about not selling her company. 'Do you want some coffee?'

'Thank you. That would be lovely.'

And his smile wasn't in the least bit smug or triumphant. It was just…nice. And it made her spine tingle.

'I'll make it, if you like.'

Had her hearing system just gone wrong? The man was used to women hanging on his every word. He hadn't even been invited here and yet he'd walked in. And now… She blinked. 'You're offering to make coffee?'

'Is there something wrong with the idea of a man making coffee?'

Ouch. She'd just been sexist and he'd called her on it. Fairly. 'I guess not.'

'Don't make assumptions,' he said softly. 'Especially if you're basing them on what the press says about me.'

Was he telling her that he wasn't the playboy the press suggested he was? Or was he playing games? Brandon Stone flustered her. Big time. And she couldn't quite work out why. Was it just because he was so good-looking? Or did she see a tiny hint of vulnerability in his grey eyes, showing that there was more to him than just the cocky, confident racing champion? Or was that all just wishful thinking and he really was a shallow playboy?

What she did know was that he was her business rival. One who wanted to buy her out. She probably shouldn't even be talking to him.

On the other hand, if Triffid didn't get that contract to her and the bank carried out its threat of calling in her overdraft, she might be forced to eat humble pie and sell McKenzie's to him, no matter how much she'd hate it. Short of winning the lottery, right now she was all out of ideas.

'So where's the coffee machine?' he asked.

'The staff kitchen's next down the corridor on the left as you go out of the door,' Stephanie said. 'The mugs are in the cupboard and so are the coffee pods.'

'Thank you.' He smiled at her, and turned to Angel. 'Cappuccino, no sugar, right?'

She nodded. 'Thank you.'

'How do you like your coffee, Stephanie?' he asked.

His courtesy made Angel feel a little bit better about Plan C. If he treated junior staff well rather than ignoring them or being dismissive, that was a good sign for the future if he did end up taking over McKenzie's. Maybe he wasn't as ruthless as she feared, despite his family background. Or maybe he just wanted her to think that.

'I'm not drinking coffee at the moment,' Stephanie said, and rested her hand briefly on her stomach.

Angel could see from the change in Brandon's expression that he'd noticed the tiny gesture, too, and realised what it meant. Stephanie was pregnant. Was it her imagination, or did she see pain and regret flicker briefly over his expression? But why would a pregnancy make him react like that?

None of her business, she reminded herself.

'What can I get you, Stephanie?' Brandon asked.

'Fruit tea, please. There's some strawberry tea in the cupboard.'

He smiled. 'Got you. Is it OK to leave my basket here on your desk for a second?'

'Sure,' she said.

As he walked out, Stephanie mouthed to Angel, 'He's *nice.*'

Yeah. That was the problem. He wasn't just an arrogant playboy. There was another side to Brandon Stone—a side she could let herself like very, very much. Which made him dangerous to her peace of mind.

* * *

Brandon returned to Angel's office, carrying three mugs. He put Stephanie's strawberry tea on her desk, then picked up the picnic basket. 'Are you sure you don't want to join us, Stephanie?'

She went very pink again. 'No, but thank you for asking.'

'Is it OK to put the coffee on your desk?' he asked when he followed Angel through to her office.

'Sure.' She looked surprised that he'd asked. Did she have a downer on all men? That would explain why Gina hadn't been able to find any information about Angel dating anyone. But she was reportedly close to her father, so maybe it wasn't *all* men. Maybe someone had hurt her badly and she hadn't trusted anyone since.

And how weird was it that the thought made him want to bunch his fists and dispense a little rough justice to the guy who'd hurt her? Angel McKenzie seemed quite capable of looking after herself. She didn't need a tame thug. Besides, Brandon didn't settle arguments with fists: there were much better ways to sort out problems.

Angel made him feel slightly off balance, and he couldn't work out why.

He scanned the room. Her office was super-neat and tidy. There were photographs on the walls; some were of cars he recognised as being iconic McKenzie designs, but there was also a picture on her desk of a couple who were clearly her parents, and one more on the wall of someone he didn't recognise but he guessed had something to do with the business—maybe her grandfather?

He unpacked the picnic basket, put the bread on a plate and cut a few slices, then handed her a plate and his other sharp knife. 'Help yourself to cheese.'

'Thank you.'

'It's not much of a choice, but I wasn't sure if you were a vegetarian,' he said.

'No, though I do try to do meat-free Mondays.' She paused. 'It's nice of you to have brought lunch.'

There was definitely a hint of suspicion in those beautiful violet eyes. She was clearly wondering what he wanted, because there was no such thing as a free lunch.

He wasn't quite sure he could answer her unasked question. He wanted McKenzie's. That was the main reason he was here. But he also wanted her, and that threw him. 'Think of it as a sandwich at your desk,' he said.

She took a nibble of the cheese and then the bread. 'A very nice sandwich, too.'

'So who are the people in the photographs?' he asked.

'The one on the wall over there is my grandfather Jimmy, back in the early days of McKenzie's.' She gestured to her desk. 'My mum and dad, Sadie and Max.'

Just as he'd guessed; but there were no pictures of Esther, who'd been at the centre of the rift between Barnaby Stone and Jimmy McKenzie. He wondered if Angel looked anything like her. Not that he was going to ask. He kept the conversation light and anodyne, then cleared away when they'd both finished.

'So,' he said. 'We managed to have a civilised meal together.'

'I guess.'

'We've done breakfast and lunch.' But the next words out of his mouth weren't quite the ones he'd intended to say. 'Would you like to come to a gala dinner with me?'

CHAPTER THREE

ANGEL REALLY HADN'T expected that, and it flustered her. 'You're asking me on a date?' she queried, hoping she looked and sounded a lot calmer than she felt.

'I guess so,' he drawled.

'No.'

'Why?'

Because gala dinners tended to be noisy and she found it wearing, having to make small talk and being forced to concentrate really hard to hear what people said.

Plus Brandon Stone dated a lot and he wasn't the serious type. She didn't want to get involved with him, professionally or personally. 'You're a Stone and I'm a McKenzie,' she said finally.

'"A rose by any other name would smell as sweet."'

'Don't quote Shakespeare at me.'

He raised his eyebrows. 'I thought you were an engineer?'

'I did *Romeo and Juliet* for GCSE. Besides, doesn't everyone know that line?'

'Maybe. So are we Montagues and Capulets?'

She scoffed. 'I have no intention of swooning over you on a balcony. Or drinking poison. And,' she pointed out, 'at thirty, I'm also more than twice Juliet's age.'

'Ouch. Thus speaks the engineer.'

'And that's why I don't want to date you. You'd spend all evening either flirting with me or making smart, annoying remarks.'

'Firstly,' he said, 'you're meant to flirt with your date.'

'Flirting's superficial and overrated.'

'Clearly nobody's flirted properly with you.'

That was a little too near the mark. 'I don't need to be flirted with.'

He held her gaze. 'No?'

'No.' She looked away.

'When was the last time you dated?' he asked.

Too long ago. 'Wasn't that in your dossier?' she retorted.

'Now who's making the smart remarks?'

At her silence, he continued, 'The gala evening is a charity dinner. The proceeds go to help the families of drivers who've been hurt or killed on the track.'

Was he trying to guilt her into agreeing? It was for a cause she knew was close to his heart, given that his brother had been killed; and it was a cause she'd be happy to support. But going to a posh dinner with Brandon, where she'd have to dress up and she'd feel totally out of place among all the glamorous socialites...

He sighed. 'At least think about it.'

She made a noncommittal noise, which she hoped he'd take as meaning 'maybe' and would back off.

Brandon was furious with himself. There were plenty of women who'd love to go to the gala dinner with him, so why was he spending this much effort on someone who'd made it quite clear that she didn't want to go anywhere with him?

He should never have mentioned the gala dinner.

He should've stuck to business.

At least if they'd been talking about cars, they would've

had something in common. Maybe that was the way to get this conversation back on track. 'Would you show me round the factory?'

Those beautiful violet eyes widened in surprise. 'That's direct. Don't you prefer other people to look things up for you and report back?'

Maybe he deserved that one. 'I'm not spying on you, if that's your implication. Anyone who works in our industry would be itching to look round, and sit in one of your cars and pretend to be its owner.'

She scoffed. 'My cars are very affordable. If you wanted one, you could buy one. In fact, you could buy a whole fleet for the price of just one of yours.'

'If that's your best patter,' he said, 'you should sack yourself as head of sales.'

She narrowed her eyes at him. 'What do you want from me, Mr Stone?'

A lot of things. Some of which he hadn't quite worked out. 'First-name terms, for a start.' He paused. 'Angel.'

She looked as if she was warring with herself, but then finally nodded. 'Brandon. OK. I'll show you round the factory.'

Walking through the factory with Brandon felt weird. Tantamount to parading her flock of lambs in front of a wolf. Though at least she'd already warned her staff that he'd made an offer and she'd refused. She'd reinforce that later

Please let that contract come through today.

She knew that the Frost prototype was in a partitioned-off part of the factory, safely away from his gaze. But he could see the areas where the body parts were sprayed, the leather seats were hand-cut and hand-sewn, the engines were built and the final cars were assembled. If he saw the process for himself he'd understand what was so special about McKenzie's, and why she was so adamant about keeping things as they were.

'This is the Luna,' she said. 'This one's being built by Ernie and Ravi. Ernie, Ravi, this is Brandon Stone.'

Ernie gave him a curt nod, but Ravi shook his hand enthusiastically and smiled. 'I've seen you race. I was there when you won the that championship, six years ago.'

'A lifetime ago,' Brandon said softly. 'I'm on the other side of the business now.'

Ravi looked awkward. 'Sorry. I didn't...'

'It's fine.' Brandon clearly knew what the other man wasn't saying. He hadn't meant to trample over a sore spot and bring up Sam's death. He patted Ravi's shoulder briefly. 'I really like the lines of this car. Is it OK for me to have a look at the engine?'

'Sure.' Ravi popped the catch on the bonnet.

Ernie gestured to Angel to step to the side while Ravi was showing Brandon the engine. 'What are you doing, Angel?' he asked in an angry whisper. 'I thought you said you weren't selling?'

'I'm not. He turned up today. I'm showing him round the factory so he can see our processes for himself,' Angel said, 'and to prove we're not compatible with Stone's.'

'You're a good boss, lass, but you're no match for a company that ruthless.' He shook his head. 'You be careful.'

'I will.' Even though Ernie should've retired a couple of years back, Angel appreciated the fact he'd decided to stay on, training their younger staff and making sure the quality control lived up to their brand's promise. And she knew he had the company's interests at heart; he'd accepted her as his boss because he knew she paid the same attention to detail that he did, and she wasn't afraid to get her hands dirty and work on the factory floor if she was needed.

As they walked through the different stations, she could see Brandon looking intrigued. 'This is very different from the way we do things at Stone's,' he said.

'Exactly. I'm glad you see your business is completely incompatible with mine.'

He raised an eyebrow. 'I didn't say that.'

'I'm saying it for you.'

He just looked at her as if to say he knew something she didn't. She brushed off her worries by switching the conversation back to technical issues. 'I guess you need more tech in a race car than in a roadster. Doesn't its steering wheel alone cost as much as we charge for a basic Luna?'

'There are a lot more electronics in one of our steering wheels than in a Luna's,' he said, and she noticed that he avoided the question. 'Maybe you should come and take a look at our place in Oxford and see how we do things.'

See where he planned to change her beloved hand-built into mass-produced monsters? She fell back on a noncommittal, 'Mmm.'

'Thanks for showing me round,' he said as she walked him back to the reception area. 'But, before I go, I thought you might like to see my favourite car ever.' He took his phone from his pocket and showed her a photograph of a gorgeous iridescent turquoise car with outrageous tail fins.

She recognised it instantly as her own favourite car. Did he know that from his dossier? Was he playing her? 'That's a McKenzie Mermaid. My grandfather designed it in the early sixties.'

'I know.'

She narrowed her eyes at him. 'I would've expected you to prefer one of your own family's cars, or one of the classic 1960s sports cars.'

'I like the classics,' he said, 'but I fell in love with the Mermaid when I saw a picture of it as a kid.'

It had been the same for her. If only there had been more than a hundred of them ever produced. The only one she'd ever seen had been in a museum, years ago, and even the fact that she was a McKenzie hadn't been enough for the curators to allow her to touch it, let alone sit in it. And because Mermaids were so rare they almost never came up for sale.

His next comment floored her completely. 'Which is why I bought one, six years ago. After I won the championship race.'

She stared at him, not quite believing what she was hearing. 'That picture... Are you telling me that's actually *yours*?'

'Uh-huh. It was a bit of a mess when I first saw it. It'd been left in a barn for years. There was more rust than anything else, and mice had eaten their way through the leather.'

'So you picked it up for a song.' That figured.

'Actually, I paid a fair price,' he said.

Why did she suddenly feel so guilty? She pushed the thought away. All her life, she'd been told that Stones were ruthless asset-strippers, and what she'd read in the business press had only confirmed that. Hadn't Barnaby walked away from the original company with way more than his fair share?

'I thought about having it restored here,' Brandon continued, 'but then I decided it'd be too much like rubbing your dad's nose in it, a Stone asking a McKenzie to restore one of their most iconic cars.'

Which was a fair point: but, actually, her father wouldn't have minded. He would've loved the chance to get his hands on a Mermaid.

So would she.

And then she thought about what he was telling her. 'So you're saying the factory at Stone's restored it?'

'No. I did it myself at home. Little by little, over a few months.'

If he'd restored it himself, by hand, that mean he had to understand craftsmanship. Everything from the precision of the angles in the spokes of the chrome wheels through to the cut of the leather in the seats and the walnut of the dash.

'Do you want to see it?'

Absolutely. Though she knew better than to appear too eager. 'And the price of seeing it is going to this gala thing with you?' She still couldn't work out why he even wanted her to go with him to a gala dinner. He had a string of super-glamorous women queuing up to date him. Why would he want to date a nerdy engineer?

Though she already knew the reason for that: one particular nerdy engineer who happened to head up his rival company, and whom he was trying to charm into selling to him.

He didn't answer her question. 'I drove over here in it today.' He shrugged. 'It's sunny. The perfect day to drive a Mermaid.'

Along a coast road, with the roof down and the radio playing upbeat early sixties' pop tunes, and he'd be wearing the coolest pair of sunglasses in the world, looking sexy as hell. Like a young Paul Newman, albeit with longer hair and grey eyes instead of blue. She could imagine it all too easily.

To stop herself thinking about that, she asked, 'You *really* own a Mermaid?'

'Don't you?' he parried.

'Unfortunately not,' she said dryly. 'Are you going to tell me that you have every single model that Stone's ever produced?'

'We have all bar one of them, actually,' he said, making her wonder which one he was missing. 'We have a museum at the factory. They're all on display.'

Something she would've loved to do here, too. But they couldn't afford the building for a museum, let alone the cars to go inside. Her dad had sold off most of his personal collection to prop up the business during the last recession, and she knew how much it had hurt him.

'Come and see the Mermaid,' Brandon said, giving her the most sensual smile she'd ever seen. Her knees almost buckled. That smile; and her grandfather's iconic design. How could she resist such a combination?

The paint sparkled underneath the sun, looking even more gorgeous than the car she'd seen all those years ago in the museum. 'It's so pretty.' Her hand went out instinctively to touch the paintwork; then she stopped herself.

'I don't mind touching,' he said.

For a second, she thought he meant touching *him*, and she went hot all over at the thought.

But of course he meant the car.

'It's the iridescent paint,' she said. 'It actually shimmers in the light.'

'That's what I loved about it, too. When I was little, I thought it ought to be an undersea car.'

So had she.

Unable to resist the lure, she ran her fingers over the bodywork. 'It's a lovely finish.' Given what he'd said about the rust, he would've had to respray it, but she could barely tell what was original and what was new. She bent down to inspect the wheels. 'And the chrome's perfect.' She ought to give credit where it was due. 'You did a good job.'

'Thank you.' He popped the catch on the bonnet. 'I guess you'd like to see the engine?'

'Yes. Please.' This time, she couldn't quite contain her eagerness.

And it was everything she'd hoped it would be. She skimmed the lines of it, memorising every detail. When she'd looked her fill, she put the bonnet back down again. 'Thank you,' she said. 'That was a really kind thing to do.'

'I'm not your enemy, Angel.'

His voice was low and husky, and his eyes had grown so dark they were almost black. For a moment, she thought he was going to kiss her. Worse still, she actually wanted it to happen. Her mouth tingled, and she felt her lips parting ever so slightly.

How ridiculous was she to feel disappointed when, instead, he took a step back?

Then he handed her the keys. 'Want to take it for a spin?'

She couldn't quite believe this. 'Seriously?'

'Your grandfather designed this car. In your shoes, I'd be pretty desperate to drive it.'

She was. And she didn't need a second invitation. She slid into the driver's seat. 'It's perfect. 'Though I could do with being a few inches taller,' she added ruefully.

'That's the thing about vintage cars. Fixed seats.' He gestured to the passenger seat. 'May I?'

'It's your car,' she said. 'Is it OK to take it round the test track?'

'The place where it was driven for the very first time? I like that idea.'

She drove the Mermaid very, very carefully over to the test track, a long thin right angle around two sides of the factory land. And then very, very carefully she drove it along one of the straights.

He smiled. 'It's a Mermaid, not a snail. You can put your foot down a bit if you want.'

Suppressing the urge to yell, 'Whoo-hoo,' she grinned and did so.

Driving this car was just like she'd always imagined it would be, with the wind whipping through her hair and the sun warming her skin. The wooden steering wheel felt almost alive under her fingers, and driving round the racetrack made her feel full of the joys of summer. The speed, the sound of the engine, the scent of the pine woods around the edge of the track... This was perfection in a single heartbeat.

Brandon had been pretty sure Angel would like the car and it would make her talk to him—but he was gratified that she liked it this much. Her hair was streaming behind her as she put her foot down along the straight, and she was laughing as she hurtled the car round a hairpin bend. She clearly loved this as much as he'd once loved racing cars. He'd forgotten that feeling. He'd barely been out in his garage, tinkering with his private collection of classic cars, since Sam died; he certainly hadn't added to the collection. But being in the passenger seat beside her reminded him of the sheer joy he'd once found in driving.

He was still catching his breath when she'd done a second lap and brought the car gently to a halt, not sure whether it was the thrill of the speed or the thrill of seeing quiet, serious Angel McKenzie all laughing and lit up and knowing that he was the cause of that smile.

And then he knew exactly what to do.

'This gala dinner,' he said.

The look on her face told him she thought he'd only let her drive the Mermaid to soften her up.

'Here's the deal. You and me—we race for it. If you win, I shut up about it. If I win, you go to the gala with me.'

CHAPTER FOUR

IF ANGEL WON the race, Brandon would leave her alone. If he won, she'd have to go to the gala dinner with him.

It was tempting. She knew the track like the back of her hand, and she knew her car even better. On paper, she should win the bet pretty easily. Yet, on the other hand, Brandon had won several championship races and he'd almost been the world champion. Twice. Even though he didn't know the track at McKenzie's, there was a risk that she was underestimating him very badly. He'd be able to drive pretty much any car, on any track, and he'd acquit himself well even if it was the first time he'd got behind the wheel of that particular model.

'Are you talking about driving side by side, or a time trial?' she asked.

'Your choice.'

'Time trial,' she said, 'and we use the same car. My Luna.'

'Nought to sixty in six seconds and a top speed of one hundred and seventy miles an hour,' he said.

She could just imagine him as a little boy, earnestly learning all the stats of his favourite cars. Funny how endearing she found it. Though she wasn't going to underestimate him—or play unfairly. This was going to be done strictly by the book.

'But I know the track and the car really well,' she said. 'Which gives me an unfair advantage. I should give you a ten-second lead.'

'And I spent years working as a racing driver,' he said, 'which gives me an unfair advantage. Especially as you've just driven me round the track, so I already know where the hairpins are and where the sharp turns are.'

She noticed that he didn't talk about how good he'd been during his career, how many races he'd won and his two world championship bids. He'd stuck to the facts rather than taking the opportunity to boast, and she rather liked that. 'I guess the advantages cancel each other out,' she said.

'We'll do three laps,' he said. 'Do you want to count just the time of the fastest lap, or average the times out over the three laps?'

Go for broke, she thought. 'The fastest. And we'll toss a coin for who goes first.'

He pulled a coin out of his pocket. 'Heads or tails?'

'Heads.'

He spun the coin, then caught it mid-air and slapped it down on the back of his hand. 'Heads,' he said, showing her.

His hands were beautiful.

Which was ridiculous. She was supposed to be thinking about the race, not about Brandon Stone's hands and what they might feel like against her skin. And since when did she fantasise about men anyway? There wasn't time to think about anything else except her work. Especially now, when she was trying her hardest to save her family business. She needed to concentrate. 'OK. The track's one and three-quarter miles long. We'll do three laps in the Luna, timing each one, and whoever does the fastest lap wins.'

'Agreed,' he said.

'Do you need to borrow a helmet, overalls or gloves?'

He smiled. 'This is a road car, so no. But if you're happier in a helmet, overalls and gloves, that's fine by me and I'm happy to wait while you get ready.'

'No.' She wrinkled her nose. 'Sorry. That was a stupid thing to ask. This isn't like professional driving. Of course you don't need racing driver stuff.'

'So do you have a transponder on the front of your car for timing the laps?' he asked.

She shook her head. 'Our test track isn't an officially accredited racing track. Yes, it's smooth enough for us to test that the car performs at high speed, and the bends are sharp enough for us to test the steering, but we tend to do lap timing here the same as we do everything else: the old-fashioned way. With a stopwatch.'

He took his phone from his pocket. 'OK. Are you happy to use my phone as the stopwatch, or would you rather use yours?'

'Yours is fine. Let's do this.'

It didn't really matter whether she won or lost. The important thing was that McKenzie's carried on. And, if the worst happened and she ended up having to sell the business to Brandon Stone, she wanted to convince him that he didn't need to change the way McKenzie's built their cars. If that meant meeting him on his own terms and acquitting herself well enough in the race to make him respect her opinion, so be it.

She ignored the other thing riding on their bet, because he couldn't possibly be serious about wanting to date her.

Butterflies did a stampede in her stomach as she led him over to her car. And again that was weird, because this was work—kind of—and she was always confident about her work. Maybe it was just adrenaline because of the race. She didn't want to think of any other reason why her heart was beating faster.

'I thought you'd pick grey,' he said, gesturing to the car's paintwork.

'Because it's mousy and boring?' The words were out before she could stop them.

'No. Because it's classic, understated—and usually underestimated.'

Was he saying that he thought she underestimated herself, or that she was trying to make him underestimate her? She didn't want to ask for clarification, because she wasn't sure she wanted to know the answer.

She unlocked the car and he climbed into the passenger seat. She could feel him assessing the car as she drove them back to the test track.

'If you want to know which options I chose,' she said, 'it was to have the wing mirrors and vents body-coloured, graphite spoke wheels, heated seats, air conditioning, and the touchscreen GPS.'

'So you're all about comfort and efficiency, then.' He touched the walnut dash, then grimaced. 'Sorry. I should've asked first, and I've probably put fingerprints on it now.'

What was it he'd said to her when she'd been itching to get up close to the Mermaid and touch the iridescent paint? 'It's OK. I don't mind touching.'

She gave him a sidelong glance and was gratified to see a slash of colour across his cheeks.

So did he, too, feel this weird pull between them? she wondered. Had he asked her to go to the gala dinner with him because he actually wanted to spend time with her, rather than it being some kind of tactic to charm her, soften her up and persuade her to sell McKenzie's to him?

The possibilities made her tingle.

But she rarely dated. The last thing she wanted to do

was start discussing the subject, only to find that he wasn't interested in her at all.

Better to stick to a safe subject. Cars and driving. The stuff she knew about. The stuff they had in common. There was more to this than met the eye, and she was going to be careful what she said to him.

'So you've never driven a Luna before?' she asked when she brought the car to a halt.

'No,' he admitted.

'I know you've probably driven many more different cars than I have, but I still don't think it's fair to race you without you taking the Luna round the track a couple of times first.'

'In business,' he said, 'you take your advantages where you find them.'

'In business,' she countered, 'McKenzie's has always believed in fairness.'

He gave her an assessing look. 'I'm going to assume that was a straightforward comment on your family's way of doing things and not an aspersion on mine.'

'It was,' she said. There had been enough bitterness between the two families. She wasn't planning to add to it. 'Just humour me and take the Luna round the track a few times.' She climbed out of the car.

He did the same, and moved the seat back before sliding in behind the steering wheel. He ran his fingers lightly round the polished wood of the steering wheel. 'I think,' he said softly, 'I'm going to enjoy this.'

Oh, help. Was he flirting with her again? What did he expect her to say?

She fell back on, 'Have fun,' and walked to the side of the track.

She watched him drive and noticed that he took the first lap very slowly; he was clearly thinking about the circuit and the angles he'd need to take the turns as fast as possible. The second time, he drove faster, handling the car perfectly.

Yup. It was pretty clear that she was going to lose this race.

But she was going to give it her best shot. This was her car, her track.

He did one more lap, then pulled up next to her and climbed out of the car. 'OK. Let's do this.'

Angel had always enjoyed driving, but she was surprised by the adrenaline surge as she took Brandon's place in the driver's seat. This wasn't just driving. And there was more than just their bet about the gala dinner resting on this.

She did the first lap and knew it wasn't fast enough. The second lap was worse, because she made a stupid error and had to overcompensate with the steering. The third lap, she knew she had to really give it her all—to get her angles right as she drove round the sharper turns, to ease off the throttle enough to let her make the turn smoothly, and to accelerate at the right time so she could make the most of the straights.

If she won, he'd leave her alone.

But did that mean he'd leave McKenzie's alone?

'Shut up and do it,' she told herself, and drove the very best she could on the last lap.

It definitely felt better than the previous two, but was it good enough?

She took a deep breath and went to face him.

'Your best lap was the last one,' he confirmed. 'One minute, fifteen point six seconds.' He showed her the stopwatch on his phone, so she knew he was telling the absolute truth. And it was a respectable time. Though she had a nasty feeling that it wouldn't be good enough.

'Your turn. May the best driver win,' she said.

His eyes crinkled at the corners. 'It's not just about driving.'

And why did that comment make her pulse speed up?

She concentrated hard as he drove off. His first lap was a careful one minute and eighteen seconds. Two seconds slower than her best. The next lap surprised her because it was even slower: one minute twenty.

Was he deliberately trying to lose?

If so, why? Had he changed his mind about going to the gala dinner with her? Or was he softening her up?

But then, on his final lap, his driving seemed different: much more focused, and very smooth.

The stopwatch confirmed what she already knew.

He'd won.

When he pulled to a halt beside her, she climbed into the passenger seat. 'I'm not sure I even need to show you this, but...' She handed his phone back.

'One minute, fourteen point nine seconds. So it was close. Closer than a breath,' he said.

Almost as close as a kiss....

She pushed the thought away and narrowed her eyes at him. 'Are you telling me you could've driven it faster than you did? That you were planning to let me win?'

'No. I'm saying the result was close. I don't know many people who could have driven it in your time.'

She scoffed. 'On my home track, in my own car?'

'Or on their home track of a similar length, in their own car.' He rolled his eyes. 'It was a good time and I'm trying to pay you a genuine compliment here, Angel. Why do you have to be so difficult about it?'

'Oh.' She felt a mixture of shame and embarrassment heating her face. She'd assumed he'd had all kinds of motives that he didn't actually have. 'Sorry.'

'You drove well. It's good to race against an opponent who's worth it.'

She felt herself flush even more because his grey eyes were serious. He really meant it. 'Thank you.'

Somehow they'd both twisted their upper bodies so they were facing each other, and he seemed to have moved closer.

The air suddenly felt too thick to breathe. What would it be like if Brandon Stone kissed her? Her heartbeat spiked at the thought.

He reached across and tucked a strand of hair behind her ear, and the touch of his skin against hers made every nerve-end tingle.

'Angel,' he said, his voice soft and husky and incredibly sexy.

And then he leaned forward and brushed his mouth against hers.

Soft. Sweet. Asking, rather than demanding.

Then he pulled back and looked at her.

She was unable to resist resting her palm against his face; she liked the fact that he was clean-shaven rather than sporting designer stubble to go with the rock-star effect of his hair. His skin was soft and smooth under her hand, and somehow the pad of her thumb seemed to be tracing his lower lip.

His lips parted and his pupils dilated.

Could she do this?

Should she do this?

But her body wasn't listening to her head. She closed the distance between them and kissed him back. This time, her arms ended up wound round his neck and his were wrapped round her waist.

She couldn't remember the last time she'd been kissed,

but she knew she'd never felt like this before. This hot, drugging need for more.

Time seemed to stop, and there was nothing in the world except Brandon Stone and the warmth of his body and the way his mouth teased hers: but then he broke the kiss. 'Sorry. That wasn't supposed to happen.'

So he regretted it already? It had been a stupid mistake. And she'd been the more stupid of them for letting it happen. Disappointment sagged through her, and she pulled away. 'It wasn't just you. I'm sorry, too.'

'Put it down to the adrenaline of the race.'

'Yeah.' Though she'd never actually wanted to kiss anyone senseless after driving a car round a track. Not until today.

'Thank you. It was good to drive round a track again.'

'Do you miss racing? Because you haven't raced since—' The words were out before she could stop them, and she grimaced. It wasn't fair to stomp all over past hurt. 'I'm sorry about your brother. That must've been rough.'

The worst feeling in the whole world. And nothing had been the same ever since. 'It was.' Brandon paused. She'd asked him a straight question. He'd give her a straight answer. 'And yes, I do miss racing. I occasionally take a rally car round the track in Oxford for a test drive, but it's not the same thing.'

'Why don't you go back to it?'

He shrugged. 'I'm getting on a bit, in terms of driver age.'

'You're only thirty-two.'

'Which is getting on a bit,' he said.

But the way she looked at him told him that she could see right through him. She knew as well as he did that it was a feeble excuse. Plenty of professional racing drivers carried on until at least their forties. True, you needed to be at the peak of your fitness to drive a car well, but age wasn't a real barrier.

Of course he missed racing.

But he'd seen the way his mother and his sister-in-law had fallen apart when Sam was killed. And there was always that risk, no matter how good a driver you were. Your car might malfunction and there would be nothing you could do about it. Someone else's car could malfunction and you might not have time to avoid the fallout from it.

He couldn't put his family through that again.

So, the day after Sam's funeral, Brandon had talked to his family and agreed to give it up.

It wasn't as if he was totally cut off from the world of racing. Stone's made excellent racing cars. Just Brandon happened to be making them for their own drivers and other teams rather than driving them himself.

He liked running the business, but it didn't give him the same adrenaline rush as driving. Which was one of the reasons why he wanted to develop a road car: to help himself push some boundaries and remind him that he was still alive, but without taking all the risks that came with professional racing.

He could change the subject.

Or he could give in to this weird impulse and tell her something he'd never told anyone else.

It was a risk. She could go to the press with what he told her. But he somehow didn't think she would.

'All right. If you want the truth…' For a moment, the words stuck in his throat. But then she squeezed his hand. Just once. Not in pity: he could see that in her expression. She was just letting him know without words that it was OK to talk—and that it was also OK not to talk. She wasn't going to push him.

And that made it easier to speak. 'When Sam died, I saw my sister-in-law Maria fall apart. I saw my mum fall apart,' he said. 'And I saw the fear in their eyes every time they looked at me. Sam was always the careful one out of the two of us, and he died.' And it had been his fault, though he didn't want to tell Angel that. He didn't want her to think less of him.

'I was the fearless one, so it was more likely that I'd be the one to take a stupid risk and have an accident.'

'Maybe,' she said, her voice gentle, 'but, by not driving any more, you're denying part of yourself.'

Was that the reason he always felt so restless? But he'd been restless before Sam's death, too, never finding the real contentment that Sam had found with Maria. He'd been ruthless about ending things with his dates. Three dates, and if he still felt restless he'd leave.

It had been so much worse since Sam's death, because he felt he didn't deserve the future he'd taken from his brother—love and a family. He just hadn't been able to let himself connect emotionally with anyone, so it had been easier to focus on the business and keep his relationships short.

'Surely there's some way you can compromise?'

He shook his head. 'If I drive again, my family's going to be sick with fear for the entire race. Watching it through their fingers, willing nothing bad to happen, flinching every time they hear a report of someone coming off the track. I can't do it to them.'

'So instead you're suppressing yourself?'

'Plenty of people would love my life.'

'But if *you* don't love it,' she said, 'there's a problem.'

Those violet eyes were deceptive, pretty enough to lull you into a false sense of security and letting you forget how sharp the brain was behind them, he thought ruefully.

Angel McKenzie could be seriously dangerous to his peace of mind. 'I find other ways to challenge myself.'

'Like trying to buy me out?'

'Or talk you into working for me.'

'And then buying McKenzie's.'

'Would it be such a bad thing?'

'My grandfather built up this business from scratch. If I sell, I'm letting him down, and I'm letting Dad down,' she said. 'If it was the other way round, wouldn't you feel the same?'

'I guess.' And wasn't that most of the reason why he was so insistent on buying McKenzie's? To make his family feel that he'd pulled out all the stops and restored their family honour? That in some way he'd made up for causing his brother's death? 'So what's your plan B?'

'Confidential,' she said.

He wasn't entirely sure that she had a plan B. 'You can't carry on as you are.'

'I know. I'm stubborn,' she said, 'but I'm not daft.'

He smiled. 'Your education is quite a few rungs above mine. I don't have a first degree, let alone an MA. You're the last person I'd dare to call daft.'

'You're not exactly an airhead yourself,' she said. 'You understand velocity, angles and wind speed. And you know your way round an engine.'

He'd had all kinds of compliments showered on him in the past. But this one was the most genuine—and it was odd how much it affected him. 'I guess,' he said gruffly, hoping she hadn't worked out how much she unsettled him.

And now was definitely time to change the subject. 'Have you always worn this?' He traced the edge of her ear with the tip of his finger. Mistake, because touching her made him want to kiss her again.

'No.'

'So what happened?'

She winced. 'It's a terrible story.'

'Tell me anyway,' he coaxed.

'OK. You know when you're five years old, you do some really stupid things because you're too young to think about the risks?'

He nodded. At thirty-two, he still did stupid things without considering the risks. Kissing her being his most recent one.

'Well, I was playing ghosts with my oldest cousins on Mum's side of the family—which basically meant walking around with a tablecloth over your head, waving your hands and saying, "Whoo, whoo, I'm a ghost," and pretending to be scary.'

He could just imagine young Angel throwing herself earnestly into the game and trying to be just as good at it as her older cousins, and grinned. 'It's the sort of thing Sammy and I would've done, too.'

'Because obviously I couldn't see where I was going with a cloth over my head, I walked into a table,' she said, 'and the corner hit me just behind my ear. Obviously I cried a lot, but everyone thought I'd simply bumped myself a bit hard, and we were banned from playing ghosts for the rest of the day.' She took a deep breath. 'But apparently that night a lump the size of an egg developed behind my ear and I became delirious, so my parents took me to hospital.'

Brandon frowned. 'That doesn't sound good.'

'They gave me some medicine and I was kept in overnight for observation, but I was fine. We didn't really think more of it. But after then, if I was drawing or had my nose in a book, I wouldn't hear my parents calling me. They thought I was just really focused on what I was doing and tuning them out, but a couple of years later I was getting really low marks on my spelling tests, even though I never spelled things wrong outside tests, and my teacher noticed that the words I was writing down weren't actually the ones she was reading out. They sounded like the words she was saying, so she thought I might have a problem with my hearing. She got my parents to take me for a hearing test.'

'And then they discovered you can't hear in that ear?'

She nodded. 'The audiologist said it was caused by impact damage, and my parents were horrified. They said there was no way they'd ever hit me, so they had no idea how it could've happened. Then they remembered the table incident, and the audiologist said that was the most likely cause.' She grimaced. 'My parents felt so guilty about it—even though it wasn't their fault, it was mine.'

'You were five, Angel. It wasn't anybody's fault, just an accident.' But he could guess the rest. Angel was only child and she'd still been quite young when her hearing problem had been diagnosed; no doubt her parents had overprotected her and sheltered her too much, just as his own mother had been overprotective with him ever since Sam's death.

And it also made him wonder something else. He looked at her. 'So it wasn't just because I'm a Stone that you didn't want to go to the gala with me?'

She looked puzzled. 'I'm not with you.'

'I remember what you said in the hotel restaurant about wooden floors making it hard for you to hear properly. It must be much worse at a party, where there's a constant background drone of noise from people talking.'

Her expression told him that he'd hit the nail on the head. That was precisely why Angel didn't enjoy parties.

She lifted her chin. 'You won the bet and I said I'd go with you if you won. I won't go back on my word.'

'If you're going to hate every minute of it, I'd rather not make you go,' he said.

She blinked. 'I didn't expect that.'

'What?'

'You. Being sensitive. Given how many girlfriends you go through.'

'Don't judge me by what the press says about me,' he said with a sigh. 'They like a good story, and half the time they make up quotes.'

'Uh-huh.' Though she didn't look quite convinced.

'And don't judge me by our family history, either,' he said.

'Didn't you judge me that way?' she asked.

'Fair point.' He reached over and took her hand. 'Let's agree to be nice to each other.'

'I'm not selling McKenzie's,' she warned. 'Or coming to work for you.'

He was pretty sure she'd do both. Because, from the look of her balance sheet, she didn't really have any other option. But he'd try to make it as easy as he could for her. 'That wasn't under discussion. This is about...' What the hell was it about? He'd never met a woman who flummoxed him like this enough to lose his train of thought totally. 'Getting to know each other, I guess,' he finished.

'Do we even want to do that?'

It probably wouldn't be tactful to point out that, just a few minutes ago, she'd been kissing him back, so it was pretty obvious that they were both interested.

'I want to get to know you,' he said. 'Imagine if you weren't a McKenzie and I wasn't a Stone. Look at what we have in common. We like cars. We like engines.' 'And my guess is that if we'd met without actually knowing who each other was, we might've liked each other.'

'You,' she said, 'have had more girlfriends than I've had hot dinners, so you'd get bored and dump me within a week. And I'm not interested in a relationship in any case. Right now, my focus is on my business.'

That stung. She made him sound like a tomcat. And he wasn't. He never led his girlfriends on or pretended he was going to offer them more than just fun for now. 'I don't sleep with everyone I date.'

'Even so, I'm not your type. You go for leggy models and actresses. And they're just the ones you're photographed with.' She shook her head. 'Maybe you're right. Maybe if our grandparents didn't have a history, we'd like each other. But we do have that history. Plus I'm not your type and you're not mine.'

'So what is your type?' he asked.

'That's for me to know and you to wonder.'

In other words, she didn't date. If he goaded her, she might eventually slip up and tell him what her type was. On the other hand, there had to be a reason why she didn't date. Maybe she'd had a really bad breakup, and her ex had crushed her ability to trust. He didn't want her to tar him with the same brush as whoever had hurt her.

'So currently we're at stalemate,' he said.

'You won the race. I agreed to your terms. So just let me know when and where I have to show up, and the dress code, and we'll leave it at that,' she said.

He had no intention of leaving it at that, but now was a good time to regroup. 'OK. Thank you for the hospitality.'

'You provided most of it,' she said. 'Thank you for lunch. And for letting me drive the Mermaid.'

'Pleasure.' He itched to kiss her again, but he knew it wouldn't be appropriate. He didn't want to give her an excuse to back away. Instead, he drove them back to the staff car park and parked the Luna next to his Mermaid. 'I'll be in touch, then.' His hand brushed against hers when he gave her car keys back to her, and every nerve-end tingled.

Her beautiful violet eyes had grown darker, he noticed; so did she feel it, too? Not that he was going to ask her. Right now he needed to tread carefully.

'OK. I, um… Drive safely.'

For a moment, he thought she was going to kiss him on the cheek. He even felt himself swaying slightly towards her. Ridiculous.

'Laters,' he drawled, and climbed into the Mermaid.

Though he was gratified to note that she stayed to see him drive off and she even gave him the tiniest wave as he reached the end of the driveway.

Angel McKenzie was a puzzle.

As she'd said very openly, she wasn't his type. She was very, very different from the women he usually dated. She wasn't fussed about appearances, and he'd just bet she was happiest wearing a boiler suit with her sleeves rolled up, getting to grips with an engine, or sketching out a design at a draughtsman's board.

His tour of the factory had left him in no doubt that she really loved McKenzie's, and her staff felt the same way about her. Ernie, the older guy who'd obviously worked out who Brandon was and didn't approve of her fraternising with the enemy, had looked concerned about her when he'd talked to her while Ravi showed Brandon the Luna. Almost like a grandfather keeping an eye out for a favourite grandchild: and there really had been a kind of family feel about the place. Nothing like the way his own factory was.

He didn't think Angel's team would respond to his uncle Eric in quite the same way as they did to her. Eric would throw his weight about and make it clear that he expected everyone to toe the line he drew, whereas Brandon had the strongest impression that Angel talked to her team and gave their ideas full consideration, and explained exactly why she did or didn't run with them.

She'd sell the company to him. Her balance sheet didn't offer any other option.

But he'd need to think hard about the best way forward and how to keep her team firmly on board—and then hopefully Angel would stay, too. Because that was the one thing he was very clear on, now: he didn't just want McKenzie's. He wanted Angel as well.

CHAPTER FIVE

'YOU HAVE TO speculate to accumulate, Miss McKenzie,' the lawyer drawled.

Which was a bit tricky when you didn't have anything to speculate with. 'Of course,' Angel agreed mildly. 'But would Triffid shoot a film on spec without a distribution deal? Because then you'd have to pay the actors and the crew up front, along with location fees and costumes and props, and you'd be spending all that money without even knowing if you'd see a return on your investment. You have to speculate to accumulate, yes—but you have to speculate *sensibly*.'

'I guess,' the lawyer said.

'So you understand that I can't just take one of my teams off their production rota for cars that have customers actually waiting for them, to make more Frosts for you that you might not use at all because you might want to make further changes to the spec. It'd be a waste of time and resources for both of us.' Resources she didn't have, and she was pretty sure Triffid wouldn't pay her for anything they didn't use, even if she pointed out that they were development costs specifically incurred for them.

'Noted,' the lawyer said. 'So are you saying you want to pull out of the deal?'

'No. I'm saying that I need to work out my factory production schedules for the Frost and my other models—just as Triffid has to work out how much time they need to film at each location, and how long they need for editing, and how long they need to get the films distributed to the various screens for the launch date,' Angel said. 'So I'd like to firm up numbers and dates, and I really think we should have everything signed off by the end of the week.'

'I'll talk to my people.'

Meaning more delay? Angel forced herself to smile and hoped that the lawyer couldn't see the anxiety in her eyes. Video conference calls could be tricky, but at least then she could be sure she was picking up every single word. Phone calls, where she had to concentrate super-hard because she had no visuals to work with, left her tired and cranky.

'I'd like to firm up the PR plans, too. To agree when we do the photoshoot of the car, when we draft the press release, and if you want to give anyone an exclusive interview. Perhaps we can have that signed off by the end of the week, too? I know the Internet makes things almost instant nowadays, but the car magazines still have lead times, and it'd be great to capitalise on this over the summer.'

'I'll talk to my people,' the lawyer said again.

'Great. I'll speak to you tomorrow, then. Same time?' Angel suggested brightly. 'Because then we can all get our ducks in a row and it'll be great for everyone.' And a signed contract would keep her bank manager happy and give her what she needed to refuse Brandon Stone's offer.

'Same time tomorrow,' the lawyer agreed. 'First thing.'

Ten a.m. in LA might be first thing, Angel thought, but it was six p.m. in England and she'd already been at her desk for ten hours. 'Lovely,' she said, and ended the call.

And please let the talking go quickly, this time. No more delays. She was running everything way too close to the wire.

Stephanie came in with a skinny cappuccino and a plate of chocolate biscuits. 'Given who you've just been talking to, I'm guessing you need this.'

'Thank you,' Angel said gratefully. 'Though you should've left an hour ago.'

'I knew you were calling Triffid—that's why I stayed behind,' Stephanie explained. 'I thought you could do with this when you were finished.'

'I could. Thank you.'

'Oh, and Brandon rang while you were on the phone to LA.'

Not 'Mr Stone', Angel noticed. So he'd clearly charmed her PA.

'Can you give him a call on his mobile?' Stephanie gave her a sticky note with the number written down.

'I will. Thanks, Stephie. Go home. And come in an hour later tomorrow morning to make up for this.'

'Yes, boss.' Stephanie smiled at her.

Angel was really too tired right now to concentrate on a phone call. Instead, she texted Brandon.

Stephie said you rang.

His reply came back immediately.

Busy or can you talk?

There was her ready-made excuse. All she had to do was say she was busy. But she surprised herself by actually wanting to talk to him.

Skype? she suggested, and typed in her profile ID.

A couple of minutes later, he called her on Skype.

'You OK?'

'Just a bit tired,' she admitted. 'It's been a long day.'

'And having to concentrate on listening to someone on the phone is hard work when you're tired.'

Again she was surprised by how perceptive he was. Since when did a Stone have a soft centre like this? 'A bit.'

'OK, then I'll keep this brief. Are you busy tomorrow night?'

'Why?' she asked carefully.

'Because I have a suggestion for you. I thought we could maybe meet halfway.'

'Halfway?' she repeated, feeling a bit stupid. What was he talking about? Selling the company to him? Because there was no halfway where McKenzie's and Stone's were concerned.

'St Albans is roughly halfway between Oxford and Cambridge.'

'St Albans?' So he'd been talking about geography after all.

'There's an outdoor performance of *Romeo and Juliet* tomorrow night in the Roman Theatre of Verulamium.' He gave her the sweetest, cheekiest smile. 'I thought it might be appropriate for us.'

The two warring houses he'd once compared them to: Montagues and Capulets. He had a point. They probably ought to keep well away from each other. But that smile was irresistible. 'Can you even get tickets for the performance, this late?' she asked.

'I can get tickets. And it'll be fun.'

'Fun.' There hadn't been a lot of that in her life, lately, with all her worries about the business. She'd almost forgotten how to have fun. It was tempting: but she simply didn't have the time.

As if he guessed at the excuse she was about to give, he said, 'You work hard. An evening off will do you good— refresh you, so you can work harder the next day.' The way he looked at her made her knees go weak. 'Are you up for it?'

She ought to say no.

She wasn't meant to be fraternising with the enemy. Or letting herself think about what it might be like to date Brandon Stone properly.

But completely the wrong word came out of her mouth. 'OK.'

'Great. Apparently they have food stalls, so we can grab dinner there. I'll bring a couple of foldaway chairs for us.'

'What time?'

'It starts at seven, so I'll meet you outside the gates at half-past six?'

Which would mean leaving work early to get there on time. As she was expecting a call from the lawyers in LA at six, it just wasn't doable. 'Sorry. I can't get there by then,' she said. But it felt mean to just knock him back. He'd been thoughtful. And she did actually want to go to the play with him. 'Can you make it another night?'

'How about Friday?' he suggested.

'Our factory finishes at half-past three on Fridays.'

'So does ours,' he said. 'Then Friday would work for both of us. Excellent. Friday it is. *Ciao.*' And then he hung up.

Ciao? *Ciao?*

She should've had him pegged as corny and ridiculous. Nobody English said *ciao* nowadays. It wasn't quite old enough to be retro, and it was cheesy and... And... That smile made it so charming.

That was the problem.

With Brandon, she still couldn't be sure what was charm and what was substance. She hated herself for being so suspicious but, given their family history and his offer to buy out her company, was he schmoozing her or did he really like her? If she'd dated more, maybe she would've had more of a clue. As it was, Brandon left her in a spin.

On Wednesday night, Angel's call to LA went much better. 'I'll email the contract over now,' the lawyer said. 'We have a digital signing system. I'll send you a link, and you can sign it once you've read it through.'

Once her own legal team had read it through, to make sure there weren't any last-minute changes, she thought. 'Thank you. I will.'

'Pleasure doing business with you, ma'am.'

'And you,' she said, lying through her teeth. The delays had driven her crazy. She definitely wouldn't have been able to cope with a career in law, where the wheels ground so very slowly. Give her the straightforwardness of engineering any day: either it worked, or it didn't—in which case you could work out how to fix it.

It was nearly two hours before the contract arrived in her inbox. But she was able to open the document without a problem, and she scanned it through quickly to make sure that everything she'd agreed was roughly there.

And then she sagged in relief.

She wasn't going to have to sell the company to Brandon after all. As long as her legal team was happy with the terms, she could sign the contract, and then she'd be able to start talking about the Frost. She could work with Triffid's PR team on a teaser campaign that would have people flocking to their dealers and asking to be put on the waiting list for a McKenzie Frost, or maybe a Luna if they couldn't wait for a Frost to be built. She'd be able to offer her staff overtime if they wanted it. Expand the business, maybe. And hopefully the Frost would become the iconic design of her generation, just as the Luna was her father's and the Mermaid was her grandfather's. She'd do McKenzie's proud.

Nobody would be at the bank at this time on a Wednesday night, she knew, but she dropped an email to James Saunders saying that the contract was now in her hands and her lawyers were looking through it.

By the time she got home, she was too tired to bother cooking dinner, opting for a bowl of cereal instead. Once she'd changed into her pyjamas, she thought about her date with Brandon on Friday night. And again the ugliest question raised its head: was this a real date, or was he simply softening her up to persuade him to sell to her?

Except she didn't have to sell the company any more.

She didn't want to make a fool of herself. Even allowing for press exaggeration, Brandon had dated a lot of women. On average, she was pretty sure he had more dates in a month than she'd had in her entire life so far. He was so far out of her league, it was untrue.

Maybe she should call it off.

Or maybe she was just tired and overthinking it. Maybe she should just go and have some fun.

The next day at work, Angel was mulling about what to wear on her date. She didn't often go to the theatre. Were you supposed to dress up? Or, given that it was an outdoor production and it might get cold as the evening went on, should you dress for comfort?

A call from the bank distracted her for a little while. This time James Saunders seemed prepared to discuss her business plan, and to her relief there was no more talk about calling in her overdraft. But then her lawyer called, wanting to make a change in one of the clauses.

'I know it means you'll have to stay after normal office hours here to talk to LA, because of the time difference,' she said, 'but you're the expert on contracts. Maybe it'd be best if you liaised with LA directly, rather than me acting as a kind of postman between you and getting it wrong?' She really couldn't face any more delays and excuses to drag things out.

Finally, on Friday lunchtime, she was able to call into her lawyer's office to sign the contract and it was sent electronically to LA.

And all the worry was over at last. She didn't have to let her family down and sell the company. Triffid's PR team would talk to her next week about the shoot and interviews, and then things would start to look up in the sales department.

She finished locking up the factory at four, and then headed for St Albans.

There were a thousand butterflies doing a stampede in her stomach as she drove to meet Brandon. Was she doing the right thing, or making a fool of herself? Though it was too late to change her mind, now.

She parked the car and texted Brandon to let him know she'd arrived.

He replied instantly.

Am in the queue by the gates. Will look out for you.

As she reached the group of people by the gates, she scanned the queue for him. He clearly spotted her first because he raised his hand to her and gave her that rock star smile.

'Hi.' She could see that he had a couple of fold-up chairs in bags slung over his shoulder; and he was dressed much more casually than she was. So she'd got the dress code well and truly wrong. 'Sorry. I came straight from work.'

He kissed her cheek. 'You look lovely.'

Was that gallantry, she wondered, or did he mean it? 'Thank you. How much do I owe you for my ticket?'

'Nothing. My treat. And no strings,' he added swiftly.

'Then I'll buy the pizza,' she said firmly, not wanting to be beholden to him. 'Especially as you've already bought me breakfast and lunch.'

'I'm not totting it all up, you know,' he said.

It made her feel even more awkward. And it must have shown in her expression, because he smiled and touched her cheek briefly with the back of his hand. 'Relax, Angel. We're just going to see a play together. Have you decided which of us is the Montague and which the Capulet, by the way?'

Strange how suddenly she felt so much more at ease. 'A rose by any other name, hmm?'

'Indeed. I brought a blanket as well as the chairs, because I thought the temperature might drop a bit once the sun sets.'

Was he suggesting that they'd share the blanket? It sounded cosy. *Intimate.* And it made her feel hot all over. She just about managed to cover her confusion.

Finally they were through the gates and Brandon set up their chairs with the minimum of fuss.

'What would you like to eat?' she asked.

'The pizza smells good,' he suggested.

'Pizza it is.'

His hand brushed against hers as they walked over to the stripy tent, sending a spike of adrenaline through her. His fingers caught hers and then curled round hers. This was definitely starting to feel like a date, she thought. A real one.

They chose from the menu chalked on a sandwich board, but when they reached the front of the queue Angel didn't quite catch what the pizza guy said to her through all the chatter round her; his face was in the shadows, and his beard meant that she couldn't lip-read what he was saying.

Without making a fuss, Brandon took over the conversation and ordered their pizzas. Angel was grateful and frustrated at the same time; most of the time, she could work round her hearing loss, but sometimes it made her feel just as she had as a child: stupid and useless.

Back at their seats, he asked gently, 'Are you OK?'

'Sure.' Though he knew he'd rescued her from a struggle, so she could hardly pretend that everything had been totally fine. She looked away. 'Thanks for helping me out. Occasionally my hearing lets me down. I could probably do with a reassessment and maybe a tweak to my hearing aid program, but I haven't had the time.'

'Make the time,' he said, 'because you're important.'

Part of her felt nettled that he was bossing her about; but she could see that his motivation was concern for her. She was used to her parents wrapping her in cotton wool, and some of the team at McKenzie's—particularly the older ones—were a bit overprotective of her, but she'd put that down to them having known her since she was a toddler.

But Brandon showing that same consideration... It actually felt good that he seemed protective of her. It made her feel cherished. Which she knew was ridiculous, because she didn't need anyone looking after her: she was doing perfectly well on her own.

Angel thoroughly enjoyed the play; and it was particularly lovely to see it in the old Roman amphitheatre with minimum props, just as plays had been produced here nearly two thousand years ago.

It started to get chilly after the sun set and, although Angel tried really hard not to shiver, Brandon noticed that she was cold. He tucked his blanket round them both and slid his arm around her.

'Do you want me to get you some hot chocolate?' he asked.

'No, I'm fine, thanks. Don't miss any of the play for me.' A cup of hot chocolate would've been nice, but she had to admit to herself that she much preferred sitting there with his arm round her.

She knew he'd chosen *Romeo and Juliet* as a nod to the rivalry between their own families; but there was a serious side to the issue, too. She had no idea how her parents would react to the idea of her dating him, or how his family would react to him dating her. On balance, as long as he treated her well, she was pretty sure that her parents wouldn't mind that he was a Stone. The rift between their families had happened seventy years ago, so it was way past time that the breach was healed.

But would his family mind that she was a McKenzie? Would they welcome her, or would they mistrust her? Especially as Brandon was now their only child?

She pushed the thought away and concentrated on the performance.

Sitting here with his arm round Angel, snuggled together under a blanket, felt oddly domestic. Brandon knew he ought to be running a mile. Domestic wasn't in his vocabulary.

But this was actually *nice*. He liked being with her. And that really surprised him.

This whole thing had been supposed to be a way of getting under her skin and talking her into doing what he wanted. But Brandon had a nasty feeling that he'd miscalculated this badly; if he wasn't careful, he could actually lose his heart to Angel McKenzie. There was so much more to her than the focused businesswoman, the engineer who did everything by the book. She was shy and sweet, and he really liked the woman he was getting to know behind her shell.

Was it possible that he was looking at this completely the wrong way round—that maybe he should be dating her properly and just forget about the business? The whole idea of dating someone seriously scared him: he'd backed away from it for so long, and a large part of him thought he didn't deserve to be loved. But for the life of him he couldn't think of an excuse to pull away; if he was honest with himself, he didn't want an excuse. And at the end of the play, when he had to pack away the blanket and the chairs, it felt a real wrench to move away from her.

He covered his confusion by playing the clown, just as he'd always covered his nerves when racing by making everyone else laugh. '"A rose by any other name would smell as sweet."' He looked at her. 'A Stone by any other name would…' He wrinkled his nose. 'The only thing I can think of would sound wrong if I said it. I'm not meaning to be smutty.'

She grinned, picking up what he hadn't said. 'Sandstone's soft.'

He gave her a pained look. 'Please.'

'Best leave it to Shakespeare,' she advised, laughing.

Like this, she was irresistible. Those eyes. If they were anything like her grandmother's eyes, he could quite understand now why his grandfather had totally lost his head over his best friend's girl.

Worse still, he found himself holding her hand when he walked her back to her car. Just as if this was a real date.

'Thank you for this evening,' she said. 'I really enjoyed it.'

'Me, too.' And to his horror he realised that he meant it. It freaked him slightly when he realised that he couldn't take his eyes off her mouth. A perfect rosebud.

For pity's sake, what was wrong with him? He didn't do soppy, and he always kept that little bit of distance between himself and his girlfriends.

The last thing he should do right now was kiss her.

Yet it was inevitable. With her looking up at him like that, all cute and soft and sweet, he simply couldn't resist dipping his head to brush his mouth against hers. Or to hold her: she was so soft and warm in his arms. The perfect fit.

One kiss wasn't enough, and he knew this shouldn't be happening, especially when she kissed him back. He never, but never, let himself get deeply involved.

Angel was the one who broke the kiss, and Brandon was actually shaking. What on earth was wrong with him? Had he gone insane? He needed to keep control of the situation. Not seeing her wasn't an option, at least not until she'd agreed to sell the business. But maybe he'd be able to be more in control of himself on his home territory.

'Can I see you again?' he asked.

She actually blushed, and Brandon wanted to pick her up, carry her off somewhere very private and make her blush even more. This really, really wasn't good.

'When were you thinking?' she asked.

My house. Now. And breakfast tomorrow morning.

He stopped himself saying it. Just. 'Next week. You showed me round McKenzie's, so I thought maybe you'd like to come to Oxford to see how we do things.'

'So I get a private tour of this famous museum of yours? I'd like that.'

His mouth was really on a roll. 'And maybe you'd like to take one of our cars round a track.'

She blinked. 'I'd be driving an actual racing car? The one whose steering wheel costs more than a whole one of my cars?'

'It'd be a rally car, if you want to drive,' he said. 'Or we have a two-seater racing car we use for "experience" days. I could drive you.'

And why on earth had he said that? He didn't drive racing cars any more.

'I'd like that,' she said.

Too late. He couldn't back out of it now. Not without explaining—and all of a sudden it was important to him that she didn't think he was a lowlife. If he told her he was responsible for his brother's death, she'd think a lot less of him. Just as he thought a lot less of himself for it.

'When's your diary free?' he asked. If those violet eyes were focused on her phone screen rather than his face, he might have a chance of getting his common sense back for long enough to deal with this properly.

To his relief, she took her phone from her bag and checked her diary. 'I've got a couple of meetings I can move on Wednesday.'

'That works for me,' he said, knowing he could ask Gina to move things around in his diary. 'Wednesday it is.'

'OK.' She looked awkward, as if wondering what they did now.

He knew what he wanted to do. He also knew it wouldn't be sensible. 'I'd better let you go. The traffic could be bad,' he said.

'Yes.'

'Text me to let me know you got home safely?' And again, where had that come from? It was more than just polite concern. He really wanted to know she was home safely.

'I will. You, too.'

And that was weird, too. He wasn't used to his girlfriends being concerned about him. It should make him want to run a mile, especially as he'd given up driving racing cars to stop his family worrying about it. He'd told himself for years that he didn't want to feel trapped by other people's emotions. But it actually felt nice that someone else cared what happened to him.

He waited for her to get into her car and drive off before he went to find his own car, but it made him antsy. Why on earth did waving goodbye to her make him feel as if he ached physically? Was he actually *missing* her? And all this after a first official date that he'd organised so casually that it wasn't supposed to be a *date* date.

And yet he'd held her hand. Snuggled with her under a blanket. Kissed her goodnight.

Somehow he was going to have to get himself under control. This was all about getting her out of his system and talking her into selling to him. Nothing more than that.

Nothing at all.

CHAPTER SIX

THE FOLLOWING WEDNESDAY morning, Angel drove to Oxford. The rush-hour traffic on the M25 kept her too busy to think about the stupidity of what she was actually doing—practically going into the lion's den.

She was still trying to work out whether she and Brandon were actually dating or not. She didn't have a clue about the etiquette of dating; as a teen, she'd been so shy that nobody had ever asked her out. She'd developed an unfair reputation as an ice maiden at university, so she knew that the men who'd asked her out had seen her as a challenge rather than actually wanting to date her, and were probably boasting about it to their friends; she'd turned them down.

After her Master's degree, she'd concentrated on work; dating Brandon was out of her comfort zone. She was surprised to realise that actually she was a little bit nervous about today. How ridiculous. Brandon had invited her here to see round the factory. She needed to think about this as business.

When she arrived at Stone's, the first thing she noticed was that the site was much larger than her own. But then again Brandon's business was more diverse than hers; as well as making the cars here, there was an accredited race track which she knew was used by other local manufacturers, and he'd talked about the museum next to the factory.

Though it set her to thinking that this was how McKenzie's could be. And maybe diversifying the business a little might help with cash flow. She definitely needed to think about how they could make the most of the Frost—an exhibition, maybe an experience day where people could drive a Frost…

But first she needed the money from the contract to come through from Triffid. And if that took as long as the paperwork had, her bank manager would be nagging her again.

She parked her car where the man on the security gate had directed her, but before she had the chance to call Brandon to let him know that she'd arrived, he came walking over to her.

In a dark grey suit and with his hair brushed back from his face, he looked every inch the businessman.

So would today be all about business?

Or would he kiss her again? Because he didn't just look like a businessman. He looked sexy as hell, with that perfectly cut suit and crisp shirt and understated tie.

She pushed the thought away. She wasn't even sure what she was really doing here anyway. He was out of her league and she'd better remember that.

'Thanks for coming,' Brandon said as she climbed out of her car.

He smiled at her, and she was cross with her knees for going slightly weak on her. Yes, he was gorgeous, but she shouldn't let herself get distracted. 'Well, who's going to turn down a personal tour of the factory of someone who's planning to be their business rival?' she asked brightly.

He coughed. 'Not necessarily rival. Where would you like to start? The museum? Coffee in my office?' Then he smiled again. 'Scratch that. You've just driven two hours to get here. Let me show you to the restroom first and sort out some coffee for you.'

When he was thoughtful like this, he was utterly irresistible. But did he know that? Was he really pleased to see her—or was he schmoozing her?

Brandon was surprised to discover how relieved he was to see Angel. He'd half expected her to call off today at the last minute, pleading pressure of work. He resisted the urge to curl his fingers round hers—after all, this was supposed to be a kind of business meeting—and led her to his office. Gina was sitting at the desk in the anteroom.

'Angel, this is my PA, Gina,' he said. 'Gina, this is Angel McKenzie.'

Gina stood up and shook Angel's hand. 'It's lovely to meet you. And you've had to drive such a long way this morning. Can I get you tea, coffee, or a fruit infusion?'

Angel gave one of those shy smiles that set all Brandon's nerve-ends tingling. 'Coffee would be lovely, thanks—milk and no sugar, please.'

'Coffee. Would that be cappuccino, latte or Americano?'

Oh, help. Gina was definitely overdoing the hospitality thing.

But Angel didn't seem in the least bit fazed. 'Cappuccino, please.'

'I'll be right in.' Gina gave Brandon her sweetest smile. 'I know how you like your coffee, sir.'

Sir? *Sir?* Oh, no. The last thing he wanted was to give Angel the impression that he was one of those bosses who insisted on being called 'sir', especially after he'd seen the way she was with her own staff.

'She never calls me that usually,' he muttered as Gina left the room. 'Do you need the restroom?'

'I'm fine,' Angel said with a smile.

Was she amused by all this? Had she worked out that his PA was teasing?

And, more to the point, how come he felt so flustered when he was on his home territory and should be feeling totally at ease and confident?

'Come through,' he said, and ushered her into his office.

The room was very neat and tidy, Angel noticed, and Brandon's desk was immaculate. Was he a figurehead, or did he just have a tidy mind?

And then she noticed the blueprint on the wall. Unable to resist, she went over to it for a closer look. 'That's a beautiful car.'

'I can show you the car itself in the museum,' he said. 'It's my favourite of all the ones we've produced. But I'm probably biased because I drove it for a couple of years.'

She looked at the date on the blueprint and realised what it was. 'The one you drove for your first world championship.'

'I didn't actually win,' he reminded her. 'I came second.'

'Which still makes you in the top two drivers of the world, that year.'

'There's an element of luck as well,' he said, 'and it depends on how the others drive on the day.'

She liked the fact that he wasn't arrogant about his success. Funny, she hadn't expected him to be humble.

Like her, he had photographs on his desk. One was clearly of his parents. The second showed a young man with a shy smile—a kind of toned-down version of Brandon, so she had a pretty good idea who he was. 'That's your brother?' she asked.

'Sammy. Yes.'

'He looks like you.' She wanted to give him a hug, but

it felt like the wrong place and the wrong time. Instead, she said, 'I'm an only child, so I can't even imagine what it must be like. But you must miss him horribly.'

'Every day.' His words were heartfelt. Then he looked shocked, as if he hadn't meant to say that out loud.

Before he could backtrack, Gina brought in coffee and a plate of posh chocolate biscuits.

'Since when have we had these in the office?' Brandon asked, gesturing to the biscuits.

'They're strictly for visitors. Mind your manners and don't have more than your fair share,' Gina said crisply.

Brandon groaned. 'Gina, can't we have *one* meeting where you're just my PA?'

'No.' Gina added to Angel in a stage whisper, 'I've known him since he was a baby. And I've changed his nappy on more than one occasion.'

Brandon put his head in his hands and groaned even more. 'I can't even sack you for being over-familiar, because my mum's your best friend and she'd kill me.'

'Exactly,' Gina said with a grin.

Angel thoroughly enjoyed the teasing; here she was seeing another side to Brandon, one with a soft centre and one she liked very much. If he'd been simply an arrogant, cocky playboy, he wouldn't have such a good relationship with his PA. Gina clearly adored him and was perfectly comfortable teasing him. And she liked the fact that at least one corner of Stone's had the family feel of McKenzie's rather than being a ruthless money-making machine.

She grinned. 'I'm glad to see I'm not the only one bossed around by my PA. Stephie's having a baby in five months and she's practising her parenting skills on me.'

Gina grinned back. 'Good for her.'

'I really like your PA,' she said when Gina had closed the door.

'Don't get any ideas of poaching her for Stephie's maternity cover,' Brandon warned.

'Because she adores you so much that she'd never leave you?'

'More like she really enjoys being my mum's spy,' he said ruefully. 'You can expect to be reported on later.'

'Is that a good thing, or a bad?' The words were out before she could stop them.

'You got the approving look—and she brought in the special biscuits I didn't even know she kept. So on balance I'd say that's a good thing.' He sighed. 'Though my mother's going to be asking a lot of questions about my intentions.'

'Parents,' she said lightly. Her own were careful not to pressure her, but she knew her mother in particular was hoping for future grandchildren.

The trouble was, Angel hadn't even met anyone she wanted to date over the last few years, since she'd taken over from her dad, let alone settle down with. Apart from going out with Brandon Stone: who was just about the worst person she could date in the first place.

To distract herself, she said, 'So tell me about your roadsters.'

'You're asking me to talk to you about confidential business stuff?'

'If someone asks me to head up their R&D department and suggests developing a new car for them, I'd kind of want to know what sort of thing they have in mind.'

'You turned the job down,' he reminded her. His eyes glittered. 'Or have you changed your mind and you're thinking seriously about it?'

She took a sip of coffee. 'That would be confidential business stuff,' she retorted.

He laughed. 'I deserved that. OK. I want a new range.

Everything from the affordable sports car—' *her* market
'—through to the top end.'

'Super-expensive?'

'Luxury and super-technical,' he said.

Which is the same thing,' she said dryly.

He gave her another of those knee-melting smiles. 'I
guess. Basically I'm looking at working with the newest
materials, and at a range of fuel options. But what I most
want is to give my clients the experience of driving a racing car. Except *safely*.'

The ends of Angel's fingers tingled at the possibilities
and she itched to start sketching.

It must have shown in her face, because he took a pad
and pencil from his desk and handed it to her. 'Feel free.'

'You,' she said, 'are not playing fair.'

'I'm not talking to Angel McKenzie, the CEO of a very
old manufacturing company who's sort of our rival. I'm
talking to Angel McKenzie, the designer. The one who
loves the Mermaid.' He paused. 'Imagine bringing the
Mermaid up to date. New aerodynamics, new materials.
Carbon fibre and titanium.'

'That's going to be seriously expensive.'

He nodded. 'And I'm looking at a good ride quality.
Maybe a different kind of suspension system.'

'So not really the Mermaid at all.'

'The feel of it,' he said. 'But brought right up to date.'

'With materials like you're suggesting, that's the opposite of what I do: making beautiful cars that ordinary
people can afford. And I can tell you now, I am *not* going
to design an affordable car for a rival company.'

'Think about the super-techy one instead, then,' he said.
'And, when you've finished your coffee, I'll show you
round the museum.'

'Deal.' She didn't touch the pencil and paper, but pictures were forming in her head as he took her over to the museum. A joint design. The first McKenzie-Stone car in years.

It was oh, so tempting.

But it would be the start of a slippery slope. One where she couldn't predict the final destination. Way, way out of her comfort zone.

The museum was a gorgeous building, light and airy. The cars were displayed well, too; even though it was clear that you couldn't touch the exhibits, you could still see everything.

'So which is the model you're missing?' she asked.

'A very early one,' he said. 'I might have sourced one. But I need to be a little more persuasive.'

'You mean, you need to offer more money,' she said dryly.

'The seller isn't bothered about money.'

'So the seller's just bothered about selling it to you? Tsk. And who was it who told me my sales patter was rubbish?' she teased.

'Yeah.' He gave her a considering look. 'Maybe we'll talk about that later. Come and see the factory.'

When he showed her round Stone's, she could see just how far apart their production techniques were. 'So your bodies are all pre-cut.'

'Precision cut,' he said.

'And put together by robots.'

'So we can pinpoint any problem immediately on the computer instead of having to wait until we do a test drive and then narrow it down—which you know can take days.'

'Uh-huh.' It wasn't the way she would want to produce a car. She liked the way they did things at McKenzie's. But she did enjoy poking around the engines in the factory and seeing just how they did things here.

'That's what I'd plan to use for the new car. Precision cutting,' he said.

'My team does precision cutting,' she pointed out. 'By hand.'

'But they haven't worked with the materials I want to work with. Not the new top-end stuff.'

The pictures flickered in her head again, and she could clearly see the new car being produced at her factory, side by side with the Frost. 'Supposing,' she said, 'you mix the old and the new. Old-fashioned craftsmanship and new materials.'

He regarded her with interest. 'Are you suggesting a joint venture?'

Was this what he'd been after all along? she wondered. And was it something that could work? Then again, now the Triffid contract was signed, McKenzie's were going to be at full capacity. She didn't have the space to produce a new car for Brandon—even though she was seriously tempted. She loved the idea he'd come up with: a cross between the Mermaid and a racing car, with aerodynamic lines.

Before she could reply, a voice boomed behind them. 'So Golden Boy's showing you round, is he?'

Angel straightened up and faced the man who'd just addressed her. 'I—er—yes.'

'Angel, this is my Uncle Eric,' Brandon said. 'Eric, this is Angel McKenzie.'

'I know who she is.' Eric's voice was full of contempt. For her, Angel wondered, or for Brandon? Or both?

She flinched on Brandon's behalf. None of her aunts and uncles on her mum's side would ever be rude to her like this, in public or in private.

'She looks like her grandmother,' Eric continued.

Ah. Was that the problem? If so, no wonder he was talking about her rather than to her.

But then he looked straight at her. 'So you've finally decided to see sense and sell to us, have you?'

Clearly he'd been discussing it with Brandon. And maybe that was why Brandon had invited her over today: for a charm offensive to persuade her round to his way of thinking. His uncle was completely the opposite of charming; hostility radiated out of him.

'McKenzie's isn't for sale,' she said quietly. She knew she really ought to be diplomatic, but that remark about seeing sense rankled so much that she couldn't just be polite and keep her mouth shut. 'But thank you for your concern about my mental state,' she added. 'I can assure that you I'm just fine.'

His eyes narrowed as he registered that she wasn't cowed by him. 'So why are you here?'

'I'm discussing possible business with Brandon,' she said. Which was true to a point. Poor Brandon, having to deal with so much resentfulness and rudeness every day.

'It looks more like he's giving you a factory tour,' Eric said. 'Golden Boy here's not bad as a factory tour guide.' He gave a nasty little laugh. 'We should probably put him in charge of the factory tours.'

And let Eric be the CEO of Stone's instead? Hardly. And if Angel had been forced to sell McKenzie's to Brandon, her staff would all have resigned rather than work for someone like Eric Stone, who blundered about totally uncaring of how the people around him felt. She smiled sweetly at him. 'A good manager understands how every job in a place fits in—so he understands the problems his staff face and the potential solutions. Plus there's a little thing called empathy. I've found it quite useful.'

'Humph,' Eric said, giving her an assessing look. 'Carry

on with the tour, Brandon.' And then, to Angel's relief, he stomped off.

'I'm sorry about that,' Brandon said, looking as if he wanted to punch the nearest wall.

And she couldn't blame him. In his shoes, she'd feel the same. His uncle had just been totally unprofessional, and it hadn't shown Stone's in a good light at all. 'It's not your fault.' She grimaced. 'I can't believe he was so rude to you.'

Brandon shrugged. 'I guess he thought he'd take over, after Dad's heart attack. He hasn't quite forgiven me for getting the top job.'

'But you've been here for three years or so. That's more than long enough for you to prove yourself. Especially as your balance sheets have improved every year since you took over.'

He raised an eyebrow. 'Been checking me out, Ms McKenzie?'

And now she was on surer ground. She'd keep this light and teasing, just as it had been before Eric's interruption. 'Pots and kettles, Mr Stone,' she parried. 'Your balance sheets are in the public domain, too.'

He smiled. 'I guess. OK. So what would you like to see now?'

'What would you like to show me?'

She regretted the question the instant she asked it, because then he looked at her mouth and she remembered how he'd kissed her in St Albans. It made her want him to do it again, and she really, really hoped he couldn't guess what she was thinking right now. 'You said something about showing me the track?' she mumbled.

'I probably should've told you to wear jeans today,' he said. 'But we can do something about that. Come with me.'

He took her over to an area with cupboards that contained bright blue overalls with the words 'Stone Racing' in white on the back, and a rack of helmets. He glanced at her shoes. 'Obviously you can drive in those?'

'Not all women wear high heels all the time, you know.'

'I'm not judging you,' he said, holding both hands up.

She grimaced. 'Sorry. I was being over-defensive.'

'That's OK—and I didn't mean to make you feel awkward,' he said. 'Find something that fits and is comfortable, so you don't get oil on your business clothes. Meet me outside through that door there—' he indicated the door at the other end of the room—'and then I'll take you round the track in the racing car.'

As soon as Brandon climbed into the driving seat, he wished he hadn't suggested this. Maybe he should've just stuck to driving her in the rally car. But she'd stood up to Eric and it had been nice to have someone bat his corner, for once. He'd wanted to show her the joy of racing round a track.

Even though it wasn't really a joy for him any more. Driving and racing was spiked with guilt.

Grimly, he brought the two-seater racing car round by the door to the changing rooms, then switched off the engine, climbed out and leaned against the car until she was ready.

She emerged a couple of minutes later in overalls and helmet. The outfit should've made her look totally unsexy, but for a moment she distracted him from his misery because the whole thing made her look so hot.

Then he remembered where they were—pretty much the last place where he could kiss her until they were both dizzy. Not unless he wanted his uncle slinging his weight around, and his mother calling him to ask him why he was kissing that nice young lady Gina had just told him about, right in the middle of the test track.

'Hey. Ready?' he asked.

'I think so.' She smiled at him. 'Would you believe I've never done anything like this?'

'Not even when someone else brought their car to your track?'

'Not even then,' she said.

'OK. You're going to be sitting very low down and the adrenaline level's going to be high, but I'm not going to show off or drive stupidly,' he reassured her. 'You'll be perfectly safe with me.'

She regarded the tyres, looking suddenly nervous. 'Slicks.'

'It's what we use in dry weather. It's the best tyre for the car. And the track's bone dry.'

'All right.' She took a deep breath. 'Let's do this.'

He helped her in and made sure her seat belt was fastened properly, then climbed into his seat. He took the first lap slowly, knowing that the seating position was very different from a road car's and could feel intimidating if you weren't used to it, and then he sped up.

Funny. He'd driven round this track so many times over the years. But it had lost its magic for him, and it felt plain *wrong* to be whizzing her round in the racing car. He'd just have to ignore it, because he'd promised to drive her in the car and it wasn't fair that she should have it spoiled by the misery that ate at him. 'Suck it up, buttercup,' he mouthed.

And he forced himself to get out of the car and smile at her when he helped her out of the back. 'So what did you think?'

'Um—adrenaline, as you said.'

'Too much?'

'Being hemmed in like this is a bit claustrophobic,' she said, 'and being this low down takes a bit of getting used to. But you're right—it was fun. Thank you.'

Fun? No. Not any more. He dredged up his best smile. 'Want to take the rally car round? You'll probably enjoy that a bit more. And this time you can drive.'

'Great. That sounds good.'

'OK. I'll take this car out of your way, first.'

Was it her imagination, Angel wondered, or had Brandon's mood changed since he'd taken her round the factory? She was pretty sure she hadn't put her foot in it, but something definitely felt wrong.

When he parked the rally car next to her, she climbed into the passenger seat before he had a chance to get out and asked, 'Are you OK?'

'Sure.' He gave her the full megawatt smile, but it didn't reach his eyes.

'Engineers are pretty good at noticing big fat lies, you know,' she said softly. 'What's wrong?'

He was silent for so long that she thought he was going to stonewall her. But then he sighed. 'I guess I owe you the truth. I've hardly sat in a racing car since Sam died. I've done the odd test drive round this track, but my heart just hasn't been in it any more.'

And yet he'd admitted to her back at McKenzie's track that he missed racing. If she asked him whether he wanted to talk about it, he might clam up—but at the same time she couldn't just sit there and watch him suffer and say nothing at all. She wanted to help him.

She reached over and squeezed his hand. 'Damned if you do, damned if you don't?'

'Something like that.' He looked anguished.

'Talk to me, Brandon,' she said softly. 'Whatever you say isn't going anywhere but me.

He paused for so long, she thought he was going to refuse. But then he swallowed hard. 'It's the guilt. It chokes me every time I get in a racing car.'

'Guilt?' she prompted, not understanding what he was talking about.

He dragged in a breath. 'Because it's my fault that my brother died.'

CHAPTER SEVEN

IT WAS BRANDON'S fault that Sam had died? Angel stared at him, not understanding.

'And that my little niece is growing up knowing her dad as just a photograph,' he continued miserably, 'instead of as the man who taught her to swim and ride a bike and made sandcastles with her and took her to the park.'

'How was it your fault?' she asked. 'You weren't driving.'

'But I should've been driving,' he said. 'The week before the race, I'd gone skiing. I'd gone on a black diamond run, showing off—and I came a bit of a cropper. I broke a rib, and that meant the officials said I wasn't fit to drive in the race, so Sam had to be my substitute.' He shook his head in apparent self-disgust. 'If I hadn't been so bratty and selfish and stupid, Sam wouldn't have been anywhere near that car—he wouldn't have been on the track at all, and he wouldn't have been killed.'

'OK, maybe I can see at a stretch that it's your fault that Sam was behind the wheel—but it's *not* your fault that the accident happened,' she said. 'What about the driver who caused the crash in the first place?'

'Micky?' Brandon wrinkled his nose. 'It wasn't really his fault. The car steering malfunctioned and there was nothing he could do about it. And he didn't exactly get off lightly. He was in plaster for months and the poor guy hasn't been able to drive professionally since.' He sighed. 'No matter how good a driver you are, you can't always get out of trouble if a car goes wrong.'

'Exactly. So the accident was just that, Brandon—a freak event that nobody could've foreseen. It *wasn't* your fault. If you'd been driving in the race, you might not even have been involved in the crash anyway, because you might not have been in exactly the same position on the track that Sam was, plus Micky's car might not have gone wrong at all. There are so many variables, Brandon. You can't blame yourself.'

He said nothing, merely grimacing.

She took his hand. 'It really wasn't your fault.'

'In my head, I can see that. But my heart's saying something different,' he said. 'I can't forgive myself. I miss him every day. I see him in the way my niece smiles, and I hate myself for what I took from her.'

And the despair in his grey eyes went deep.

Angel had no idea what to say or how to make him feel better. Wanting to convey at least some kind of sympathy—fellow-feeling rather than pity—she placed her palm gently against his cheek.

He twisted slightly so he could press his lips into her palm, and her skin tingled where his mouth touched her.

Helplessly, she slid her other arm round his neck and reached up to kiss him.

And he kissed her back as if he were drowning and she was the only thing keeping him afloat. Her heart broke for him. He'd spent the last three years convinced that he was at fault for his brother's death; how did you live with a feeling like that?

'I'm sorry,' he said when he broke the kiss. 'I'm supposed to be driving you round the circuit in the rally car.'

'It's OK. You don't have to if you don't want to.' She bit her lip. 'If I'd had any idea how painful it would be for you to get behind the wheel of that racing car this morning, I would've suggested we skip it.'

He leaned forward and kissed the corner of her mouth. 'Because you're a much nicer woman than I deserve.'

Was that why Brandon seemed to date his way through such a long line of women? Because he didn't think he deserved love, so he never stayed with anyone long enough to let them love him? Her heart broke for him just a little bit more.

'No. Because I think you're hurting enough without me adding to it,' she said softly. And she wasn't that nice. She was a coward who'd buried herself in work rather than dealing with her shyness in her personal life.

'You're nice,' he said softly.

'And you're nicer than you give yourself credit for,' she said. OK, so maybe bringing the Mermaid to show her had originally been part of a plan to talk her into selling her the company, but he'd still let her sit in it and actually drive it. He hadn't had to go that far.

'I'm not as nice as you deserve.'

She went still. Was this his way of ending their fledgling relationship? Was she about to get the 'it's not you, it's me' speech?

Then she shook herself. This wasn't about her. This was about him feeling horrible and not being able to deal with it. And she really wanted to make him feel better. 'You know what?'

'What?'

'You're a Stone and I'm a McKenzie. We're not supposed to think each other is nice.'

That earned her a wry smile. 'Maybe.'

'Sam was your older brother, right?'

He nodded.

'So I'm guessing he bossed you around?'

Brandon smiled then. 'When I was little. Before I was old enough to be stroppy and do things my way.'

'But he loved you as much as you loved him?'

'He worried about me. Nagged me about burning the candle both ends and taking risks,' Brandon admitted.

Just as she'd thought. 'I didn't know him, but from what you'd told me I'd guess that he would've been livid with you for blaming yourself for his death.'

'Maybe.'

'Definitely,' she corrected. 'And I also think he might've been sad that you'd lost the joy you once had in driving.'

'Probably.' Brandon's face was tight.

'Hating yourself isn't going to bring him back. And in the end that hatred is going to tarnish your memory of him,' she said softly. 'My dad's sister died when he was little. He always says she would want us all to remember her with smiles and focus on the good stuff.'

'But how do you do that?' Brandon asked.

'Be kind to yourself, for a start. Block out how bad you feel and think of something that makes your heart feel light.'

'That sounds,' he said, 'like personal experience.'

'It is,' she said. 'When I was a teen, I was crippled by shyness. I hated people treating me as if I was stupid and useless just because I was deaf. I didn't know how to talk to people and I clammed up. I saw a counsellor about it, and she suggested that when I felt bad, I should focus instead on something I loved talking about—engines, cars, that sort of thing.'

'And it worked?'

She nodded. 'It's as if this lump in my throat just dissolves and I can talk easily again.'

'So you had to make a real effort.'

'I didn't say it was easy,' she said. 'Just it's a method that works for me. So maybe look at what you're good at. What you love. Focus on that and distract yourself.'

He stole a kiss. 'Angel McKenzie, you're amazing.'

'I'm very ordinary,' she said. And, because the look in his eyes made her heart feel as if it was doing anatomically impossible things, she went for distraction, too. 'And I can tell you something else. Right now, you need cake.'

He blinked. 'Cake?'

'Let's go into Oxford and I'll buy you afternoon tea. Anywhere you like—I'm assuming you know where they do the best scones in the city?'

'I guess.' He paused. 'You know what would be even better, in May?'

'What?'

'How are you in boats?' he asked.

Where was he going with this? 'Boats?'

'Punting, to be precise.' He gestured outside. 'It's sunny. The river will be gorgeous today.'

'I've never been punting,' she admitted.

'What, when you live in Cambridge?'

She saw in his expression the moment he realised why. 'Your parents were worried about you falling into the river, getting an ear infection and losing the rest of your hearing?'

'Something like that,' she agreed. 'Though they didn't wrap me up in cotton wool to constrain me; they just wanted to keep me safe. Besides, if I fall in and get my hearing aid wet, it'll stop working.' Leaving her with hearing on one side only, which wasn't quite enough to let her follow every nuance of a conversation. She could manage for a couple of days, but it would be a struggle and she'd be bone-deep tired and frustrated at the end of it.

'I promise faithfully,' he said, 'not to let you fall in.'

There was enough of a smile on his face to let her know that they'd pulled back from the danger zone. She took the risk of going a little further and teasing him. 'So as well as being a super-hot racing driver, you're an expert at punting, then?'

'Honey,' he drawled, 'I'm good at everything.'

Their gazes met, and suddenly she couldn't breathe.

He was certainly good at kissing; and she went hot all over at the thought of what it would be like if they took this thing between them any further. What it would be like if they actually made love.

Except… Would she have to tell him about her woeful, embarrassing inexperience? But, if she did, maybe he'd think there was something wrong with her.

Maybe there *was* something wrong with her.

She pushed the thought away. She'd just given him a lesson on avoidance tactics. Going over the top and flirting outrageously was clearly his way of doing that.

'OK. Let me get changed and we'll do the river. And then we're doing cake,' she said.

By the time Angel had changed back into her business suit and he'd changed out of his own racing overalls, Brandon had got himself back under control. He was still shocked that he'd actually confided in her; he never talked about his feelings to anyone, especially when it came to Sam's death. Yet there was something about Angel that made him feel grounded, safe enough to talk about the dark things in his head.

That in itself was worrying. He didn't want to get close to her. This was all meant to be about getting her to sell McKenzie's to him. He was on his home ground; it should be easier to resist his attraction to her here.

Yet it wasn't.

He needed to keep this light and easy. Play on their differences. Bring up the Oxford-Cambridge rivalry, maybe, rather than the Stone-McKenzie one.

'Ready to go?' he asked, giving her his best full-wattage smile.

'Ready,' she confirmed.

'Great.' He drove them into the city and managed to find a parking space. As they passed the Ashmolean Museum, he gave her a sidelong look. 'I should probably point out the Ashmolean. We have rather better museums in Oxford.'

'Than Cambridge, you mean? Nope. Raise you the Fitzwilliam,' she said.

He was relieved that she was playing along with him, so he could push all the emotions back where they belonged—in the locked box around his heart. 'Raise you the Pitt-Rivers,' he said. 'And we have the Bodleian Library—which is one of the oldest libraries in Europe, and the second-biggest in Britain.'

'I'll give you that,' she said. 'But in Cambridge we have one of the four remaining round Templar churches in the country.'

'We have a Saxon tower in St Michael's church,' he said.

'And we have St Bene't, which also has a Saxon tower.' She smiled. 'I think we're going to have to declare a tie on that one.'

'Perhaps.' That smile was irresistible. And he really wanted to hold her hand. What on earth was wrong with him? He wasn't a teenage schoolboy. He didn't do soppy.

But something about Angel made him feel different.

Brandon managed to keep himself under control until they got to Magdalen Bridge, where the punts were all set out waiting for business. He paid for their punt, and then he glanced at Angel's business suit. Her skirt was definitely too narrow to let her clamber into the punt. 'Can you forgive me for doing something a bit troglodytish?'

She looked surprised. 'What?'

'I'm still not with you.'

He gestured to her skirt. 'Short of asking you to hike that up…' And then, before she could protest, he picked her up and climbed into the punt with her.

She felt really, really good in his arms.

But they were in public, so that was enough to stop him giving in to the urge to kiss her until they were both dizzy—which would be a stupid thing to do on a boat in any case, especially as he'd promised to make sure he wouldn't let her fall in.

'Sorry about that,' he fibbed. 'It was just the safest way of getting you into the punt.

Her violet eyes were wide with shock and the expression on her face told him she didn't think he was sorry in the slightest. It was a real effort to hold himself back from stealing a kiss.

'Take a seat, my lady, and I'll punt you down the river.'

'As long as you don't try to sell me down the river,' she said dryly.

'As if I'd even try.' He smiled at her. 'Right. Note that I'm punting from the Oxford end.'

'There's an Oxford end and a Cambridge end of a punt?' she asked.

'There is indeed. Here, we punt from the sloping end. It's also less slippery as well as being traditional.'

'Right.'

She sat on the padded red velvet seat, and he gently steered them out into the middle of the river. 'I feel as if

I ought to be wearing a stripy jersey and singing "*O Sole Mio*".'

'Oxford is hardly Venice,' she teased back.

He liked this light-hearted side of her. 'Ah, but we have a bit of Venice in Oxford, and I don't mean the punting. I'll show you later. All righty, my lady. Your tour of Oxford starts here at Magdalen Bridge.' He pointed up at the golden stone bridge with its gorgeous parapet.

The sunlight sparkled on the river Cherwell; the river looked almost as green as the trees in the summer afternoon light, and the ducks and swans were out in full force, paddling lazily between the punts.

Funny how being on the river made him feel grounded again. He'd spent so much of his earlier life trying to drive as fast as he could and stay ahead of the pack, yet the slow pace of punting and the sound of the water lapping against the banks and the sight of the swans gliding always made him feel better. Right now he really wanted to share that with her. But sharing his favourite places didn't mean he was letting her close—did it?

'And this is Christ Church College Meadows,' he said. He gestured to the golden stone building in the background. 'This is where Lewis Carroll taught when he wrote *Alice in Wonderland*.'

'It's beautiful,' she said. 'I think it'd inspire anyone.'

Even though the conversation between them lapsed, it didn't feel awkward. He liked the fact that Angel didn't need to chatter on and on—something that had grated on him with quite a few past girlfriends.

Not that Angel was his girlfriend, exactly.

He didn't want to let himself think about what she could be to him, and instead concentrated on punting, on the slow steady strokes of the pole that propelled the boat forward past the college buildings, all red roofs and mellow golden stone, and under the little white bridges.

Finally, he glided the punt into a berth at the station.

'You are *not* lifting me out of the boat,' she said.

Because she didn't want to be close to him?

Maybe the question showed on his face, because she said, 'I'm not a helpless little princess.'

No. She was independent, stubborn and bright. And he liked that about her, too.

'Can I at least offer you a hand? Simply because it's tricky for anyone to get out of a punt, and not because I'm trying to make you feel pathetic. I did promise not to let you fall in, and I don't want to break that promise.'

'Hmm,' she said.

And then she hiked her skirt up.

Not too much, but enough to let her climb out of the boat. Though she did at least hold his hand for balance. And somehow he forgot to let her hand go again.

'Cake?' she asked.

'Soon. I want to show you what I meant about Venice, first.' He took her to New College Lane. 'Behold the Bridge of Sighs.'

'Except it's over the street and not over a canal.' She looked at it thoughtfully. 'And it looks more like the Rialto than the Bridge of Sighs.'

He smiled. 'Trust the engineer to notice that. And I suppose you're going to tell me that the one in Cambridge looks more like the one in Venice?'

She grinned. 'No. It's kind of like this one: it's simply the fact that it's a covered bridge. Though at least ours is over the Cam and not over a road.'

'Noted,' he said dryly. 'Score another to Cambridge.'

She smiled back. 'So was the bridge always part of the college?'

'No, it was built in 1913 to join the two parts of Hertford College.' He smiled. 'According to legend, someone did a health survey of the colleges and the students here were the heaviest, so they closed the bridge to make the students take the stairs and get more exercise.'

She laughed. 'You're kidding!'

'Sadly, it's just an urban legend. Apparently you end up taking more stairs if you use the bridge than if you don't, and the bridge has never been closed to students.' He smiled. 'I think it'd be better if they pinched the legend from the proper Bridge of Sighs—that love lasts for ever if you kiss under the bridge at sunset.'

Love lasts for ever if you kiss under the bridge at sunset.

Angel looked at Brandon. She didn't think that he even believed in love, let alone that he thought it could last for ever.

And then she thought about kissing. Remembered what it had felt like when his lips had teased hers, the way he'd sent her pulse thrumming.

She really didn't know what to say. All the words had gone out of her head.

He was still looking at her. And she could see the second his gaze dropped to her mouth. So he was thinking about it, too...

Then he seemed to shake himself. 'Cake. We're supposed to be looking for afternoon tea.'

She seized on the suggestion gratefully. 'Yes. Tea. I take it you know somewhere?'

'Oxford,' he said, 'had the oldest coffee shop in England. Pepys mentioned it in his diary.'

She couldn't quite come up with a Cambridge quote to match that. 'So does it still exist?'

'No,' he admitted. 'But there is another café on the site. And actually I do know somewhere that does good tea.'

The café he took her to turned out to be a stunning building with pillars, lots of gold leaf, chandeliers and potted palms. The waiters were all wearing black suits and white shirts. And the high tea was delightful, a tiered plate with a selection of finger sandwiches, still-warm scones served with clotted cream and strawberry jam, tiny lemon tartlets with a raspberry on top, pistachio macaroons and tiny sticky ginger cakes studded with stem ginger.

'This is perfect,' she said.

He gave her an impish smile. 'Better than Cambridge?'

She rolled her eyes. 'As if I'm ever going to say that.'

'We're on opposite sides in so many ways,' he said.

And yet they were on the same side, too. 'Maybe,' she said, and refilled her cup with Earl Grey tea.

She'd still been thinking about his idea for an updated version of the Mermaid. And she was itching to sketch. 'Can I be rude?' she asked.

'An important phone call you need to make?' he asked wryly.

'No.' She pulled a pad and pencil from her bag. 'Give me five minutes. Drink your tea.'

Brandon rather liked Angel's occasional little flashes of bossiness. And he liked the fact that she'd asked if she could take her attention away from him for a few moments. Too many of his past girlfriends had spent a meal out checking their phones for texts or social media notifications, or taking endless selfies. He'd guess that Angel had never taken a selfie in her life.

It looked as if she was sketching, and her face was really animated as she worked. Clearly she loved what she did. And Brandon wondered when the last time was that he'd felt that kind of passion for something.

Though he knew the answer. It had been before Sam's crash. Brandon had loved driving more than anything else. Racing. Using all his skills to anticipate his competitors' moves and when to make a bid for the front spot. Seeing the chequered flag come down as he went over the line.

He'd lost that along with his brother.

And he didn't know if he'd ever get it back. If anything would ever fill the holes in his life that he didn't usually let himself think about. Angel had suggested focusing on what he loved, but the guilt still got in the way.

Angel finished sketching, then pushed the pad over to him. 'Were you thinking about something like this?'

He stared at the picture. It was only a rough sketch, but it was incredibly close to the picture he'd had in his head when he'd talked to her about the high-end car he wanted to produce.

'I was thinking teal iridescent paint,' she said, 'with chrome accents on the curves here and here.' She pointed out the areas on her sketch. 'Or we could mess about and make it two-tone—say, black and red.'

'And you kept the fins. That's going to affect performance.'

She nodded. 'I guess it depends on the angles. We can tweak the aerodynamics.'

We.

So was she going to work with him? Were they going to turn this whole thing on its head and do something new, instead of concentrating on the old Stone's and McKenzie's firms? Did this mean they'd be partners—and not just in business?

The thought made him feel dizzy.

He hadn't expected this—for them to be this compatible, to see things the same way. It scared him and thrilled him at the same time.

'A rear spoiler would work better,' he said.

'Yes, you're right. Give me a minute.' She took the pad back and did a second sketch.

Brandon couldn't take his eyes off her. Her hands were deft and sure, and he couldn't help wondering what they'd feel like against his skin. And when she was all serious and concentrating like that, she looked stunning. It made him want to lean over the table and kiss her, regardless of who was around them.

This was bad.

Really bad.

He needed to get himself back under control. He didn't *do* relationships. Falling for the CEO of his family's bitter rival would be very stupid indeed.

She pushed the pad back across the table to him. The second sketch was very similar to the first, but this time she'd drawn a spoiler instead of the fins.

'That's brilliant. Can I keep these?' he asked. And then he frowned. 'I mean for *me*. Not because I'm going to run off to another designer and ask them to work on this or anything like that.' But because working closely together, she'd made him remember how much he'd loved cars. How much he still loved them, deep down. And it was the first time he'd felt this kind of lightness of spirit in years.

She smiled. 'Sure you can.'

'Thank you.' He folded the pieces of paper and put them into his wallet.

When they'd finished their tea—which she insisted on buying, and he decided not to argue because he knew how independent she was, plus then he could claim it was his turn to pay for whatever they did next—they walked back to his car. Somehow his fingers ended up tangling with hers, but she didn't pull away and neither did he.

Weird.

He just wasn't the soppy sort.

Yet here he was, walking hand in hand with her through Oxford. He'd taken her punting. She'd bought him afternoon tea. They'd talked about their mythical joint car and come up with a first design tweak to it. And his heart felt lighter than he would've ever thought possible.

Funny how he didn't want today to end.

She just made polite conversation with him on the way back to the factory. He didn't invite her in, after he'd parked next to her car—the last thing he wanted was for Eric to appear and come out with some stupid comment and ruin the mood—but, before she could get out, he said, 'I've really enjoyed today.'

She turned to face him, her violet eyes all huge and beautiful. 'Me, too.'

'Maybe,' he said carefully, 'we could do something at the weekend. If you're not busy.' Which was a bit disingenuous of him, he knew, because she'd more or less admitted to him that she didn't have a social life.

'I'd like that,' she said, rewarding him with that gorgeous shy smile.

'Can I call you?' God, he sounded like a seventeen-year-old. The weird thing was, she made him feel like a seventeen-year-old, ready to conquer the world. When had he last felt like this—as if there was hope and light at the end of the tunnel, instead of a black hole dragging him in?

'Yes.'

He smiled, leaned forward and touched his mouth to hers. Just once, enough to remember the feel of her lips against his but not for long enough to let him lose control. 'Drive safely. Text me when you get home.'

'I will.'

He got out of his car and leaned against it, watching her drive away. Once she was out of sight, he headed for his desk.

Gina smiled at him as he walked back into his office. 'Angel not with you?'

'She's gone home.'

'I see.' Gina paused. 'I liked her.'

Which sounded to Brandon as if Gina had been talking to his mother. 'Uh-huh,' he said, trying to sound casual.

'I mean *really* like her—and I think you do, too.'

He groaned. Yes, she'd definitely been talking to his mother. 'We're not discussing this, Gina.'

'She's nice. Really nice. And I think she understands you a lot better than those clothes horses you normally date.'

She did. Which was one of the things that worried him. He didn't want to get close to her; yet, at the same time, he did. 'This wasn't a date.'

'No?' Gina scoffed.

He smiled. 'This morning was business.'

'But this afternoon was a date?'

'She hadn't been to Oxford before. We did some touristy things. As you'd do with someone you're trying to sort out a business deal with,' he said.

'Hmm,' Gina said.

Busted. But he still wasn't going to admit to it, because he really wasn't sure how he felt. Angel McKenzie was nothing like he'd expected her to be. She made him feel all kinds of things he couldn't quite pin down, and it made him feel ever so slightly out of control.

'It's purely business,' he said again, knowing that he was lying to himself as well as to his PA. 'I'll make the coffee.'

'You do that, sweetie.' Gina wrinkled her nose at him. 'It'd be good to see you happy.'

'No matchmaking.'

''Course not,' she deadpanned.

She'd *definitely* been talking to his mother. 'Coffee,' Brandon said, and fled before Gina could grill him any further.

CHAPTER EIGHT

ON FRIDAY MORNING, Brandon texted Angel.

When are you free for me to Skype you?

She really appreciated the fact that he'd remembered she preferred to speak face to face rather than struggle with the phone.

Lunchtime? she suggested. Around twelve?

OK. Talk to you then.

He was as good as his word. 'Hey. I've found something we can do this weekend.'

'What?'

'It's a surprise.'

She narrowed her eyes at him. 'I'm an engineer. I'm not keen on surprises.'

'It's something you'll definitely like,' he said. 'But it does mean staying away overnight. Is that OK?'

Overnight.

Did that mean he wanted to take things further with her—and this soon?

Her worries must've been obvious, because he said, 'I planned to book us separate rooms.'

'OK,' she said cautiously. 'As long as I pay for my own room.'

'We'll talk about that later,' he said. 'Can I pick you up at nine tomorrow morning?'

Meaning he'd have to leave Oxford at the crack of dawn? It still gave her no clue about where they were going; but she had to admit to herself that she was looking forward to spending time with him. They'd definitely become closer, this last week, and she was starting to feel comfortable with him. 'All right.'

'Good. I'll see you then.' His voice and his eyes were filled with warmth. 'Text me your address so I can put it in the satnav.'

'Will do. What's the dress code?'

'Casual. And do you have good walking shoes?'

'Yes.'

'Excellent. Bring them,' he said. 'I'll see you tomorrow.'

So they were going walking? But where? And wouldn't it make more sense for her to meet him wherever it was, rather than make him drive for two hours to her place first? Surely she was out of his way?

Though Angel was pretty sure that if she asked him straight out, he'd come up with some excuse that told her even less.

On Saturday morning her doorbell rang at nine o'clock precisely.

Brandon was wearing faded jeans, boots, and a white shirt with the sleeves rolled up halfway to his elbow and the neck unbuttoned. He looked utterly gorgeous; but he also seemed to be unaware of it rather than preening like a peacock. A couple of weeks ago, she'd had him pegged as arrogant and vain, but she was learning that he was nothing of the kind. And she really liked the man she was getting to know.

'Hi.' He leaned forward and kissed her on the cheek. 'Ready to go?'

She indicated her small overnight bag, and he grinned. 'That's another good thing about dating an engineer. She packs sensibly.'

She pulled a face at him. 'That's horribly sexist. That, or you've been dating the wrong women.'

'Probably true on both counts,' he said with a smile. 'My car's parked a couple of doors down from you.'

She set the alarm, locked the front door and followed him to what turned out to be a newish and very expensive sports car.

'How many cars do you actually own?' she asked. There was the Mermaid, the car he'd driven to St Albans, and the one he'd driven in Oxford; this made at least the fourth different one.

'I've always liked cars. And I've been lucky enough over time to afford to indulge my whims without making life hard for anyone else. It's an entirely un-guilty pleasure.' He looked totally unabashed. 'Come and see my collection some time.'

'Is that as in "come and see my etchings"?' she asked wryly.

'It wasn't a ruse to get you into bed.' He paused. 'Though now you've made me think about doing precisely that.'

That made her think about it, too, and she went hot all over. She was glad of the excuse to put her bag in the boot of his car to cover her confusion.

Brandon noticed that Angel had gone quiet on him by the time she climbed into the passenger seat, and he wondered if he'd just pushed her too far. He needed to get the easiness back with her.

'You can pick the music, if you like,' he said.

She raised an eyebrow. 'You're telling me you don't already have a driving playlist sorted out?'

'Like the compilations you can buy which have the same songs on, just in a different order? No.' He smiled. 'There is something I like to drive to, but you have to promise to sing it with me.'

She shook her head. 'I'm not a good singer.'

'Neither am I. But we're the only ones who can hear us,' he pointed out, 'so who cares?'

'I guess.'

He put on the track and gave her a sidelong glance; OK, so it was retro, but she had to know it? 'Mr Blue Sky' never failed to put him in a good mood when he was on a long business drive; hopefully it would have the same effect on her.

To his relief, she joined in, albeit a little hesitantly at first. But when he hammed up the falsetto bits of the song, she was smiling—laughing with him rather than at him. And then suddenly the easiness was back between them. They were just a girl and a guy, driving down the motorway for a weekend away, and life felt good. Enough for him to forget that he was supposed to be keeping her at a distance.

When they stopped at the service station for a comfort break, Angel asked, 'Do you want me to drive for a bit?'

'No, it's fine—unless you're tired of being a passenger?'

'I just thought you might want a break, especially as you had to drive for two hours to get to me first.'

He liked the fact that she'd considered that. His previous girlfriends had always taken for granted that he'd do all the driving. Or maybe he'd chosen them partly because he knew they'd take him for granted and wouldn't get close to him, and he'd be able to walk away from them with barely a second thought.

'I know, but I like driving.' Particularly with her, though he wasn't going to spook her—or himself—by saying it. He didn't want her to back away. Or for him to lose that feeling and slide back into the darkness again.

Finally, they turned off the main road onto a series of narrow, winding rural roads which led them through pretty Cumbrian villages.

'This is a really gorgeous part of the world,' she said, 'but where exactly are we going?'

'The satnav claims it's about half a mile further,' he said, and turned into a very long driveway.

At the end was a sprawling ancient farmhouse built of grey stone. 'Here we are,' he said when he'd parked, and climbed out of the car.

'Who lives here?' she asked, joining him.

'Bill Edwards.'

Which left her none the wiser. Why did Brandon want to visit this mysterious Mr Edwards, in the middle of nowhere? And why was he being so secretive about it?

He rang the doorbell, and an elderly man answered, a black Labrador with a grey muzzle at his heels. 'Mr Edwards? Brandon Stone,' he said. 'And this is Angel McKenzie.'

'Good to meet you.' Mr Edwards shook their hands warmly. 'Come in, come in. Martha, we need tea for our guests.' He ushered them into the kitchen and indicated for them to sit down at the scrubbed pine table; his wife greeted them and bustled round the kitchen, preparing tea.

'Is there anything I can do to help?' Angel asked.

'No, love, you sit down and relax,' Martha said with a smile.

The dog sat at Brandon's feet and rested his chin on

Brandon's knee; Brandon absently scratched behind the dog's ears, and Angel found an unexpected lump in her throat. The dog clearly liked him, and didn't they say that animals were good judges of character?

'So you're a relative of Jimmy McKenzie, Miss Mc-Kenzie?' Mr Edwards asked.

'His granddaughter,' she confirmed, 'and please call me Angel.'

'Then you can call me Bill,' he said. 'And you work in the family firm?'

She nodded. 'Dad retired a couple of years ago. I took over from him.'

'And you head up Stone's,' Bill said to Brandon.

'I do,' Brandon said.

Bill's weathered face creased with a smile. 'Well, it's a surprise you're even in the same room as each other, let alone driven all the way up here together.'

'We're...' Brandon looked at Angel. 'Friends.'

Their relationship was a good deal more complicated than that, but she wasn't about to contradict him.

'Well. It's fitting that you should come here together.'

Angel was still mystified, until after Bill and Martha had made them drink two cups of tea and eat a slice of the lightest, fluffiest Victoria sponge she'd ever tasted. And then Bill led them outside.

'Here she is,' he said with pride as he ushered them through a door.

Angel blinked as she saw the ancient car sitting in the garage. 'Is that what I think it is?'

'Did Brandon not tell you he was bringing you to see it?' Martha asked.

'No. I wanted it to be a surprise,' Brandon explained.

'I can't quite take this in. That's the first McKenzie-Stone car,' Angel said. 'I've only ever seen photographs of one. I wasn't even sure there were any left in existence.' And to see one in such perfect condition, obviously well loved, was incredible.

'Brandon here's been trying to persuade me to sell it to him for months,' Bill said.

And then she understood. This was Brandon's 'missing' car from his collection. The one he wanted for the museum at Stone's. He'd said that the owner couldn't be persuaded to sell by offering more money; clearly he'd hit on a strategy that he thought might be rather more effective.

Using her as a kind of leverage.

Bitterness filled her mouth, but she forced herself to smile. 'It's lovely to see it, and especially in such amazing condition. So have you had it for very long?'

'It's been in the family since day one,' Bill said. 'My grandfather bought one of the first ones they ever made, and he handed it down to my dad, who handed it down to me.' He looked regretful. 'Me and Martha, we lost our lad when he was tiny, or it would've gone to him.'

'I'm sorry,' Angel said.

'No, lass, don't cry for us. We've had a good life,' Bill said. 'But our nephew, he's not really one for classic cars. He'd rather have the money to use on some newfangled equipment for the farm. And it's time this old girl went somewhere she'll be appreciated.'

'Brandon will look after her properly,' Angel said. Even though she was furious with him for using her to get his own way, she couldn't deny that he'd do right by the car.

'It was a shame they didn't make more,' Bill said. 'But your grandfathers fell out.'

'Yes.' And she and Brandon would be having a big falling-out, once they'd left here, she thought crossly. 'It's a shame that they let love get in the way. I didn't really know my grandparents, but my mum once let it slip that Esther really regretted the rift between Jimmy and Barnaby. I think she wanted to do something to heal it.'

'But I think both our grandfathers were too stubborn to make the first move,' Brandon said.

'Something like that,' Angel agreed. Before today, she'd thought that maybe she and Brandon could change things and heal the rift between their families. But maybe not. She'd believed that he'd wanted to go away for the weekend with her, whereas clearly he'd seen this whole thing as a business opportunity. He'd opened up to her in Oxford, or so she'd thought; but maybe he'd just been playing her all along. What a naive, stupid fool she was. He was a Stone. Ruthless to the bone.

'You came here together to see the car,' Bill said thoughtfully. 'Does this mean there could be a new McKenzie-Stone car in the future?'

The car she'd sketched for Brandon. Their joint idea.

That definitely wasn't going to happen now.

Before she could open her mouth to say no, Brandon said, 'We're talking. Which is more than our families have done for decades.'

'And that's a good start.' Bill held out his hand. 'I'll sell the car to you, Brandon. It's a deal.'

Brandon shook his hand warmly. 'Thank you. I'll take good care of it.'

'I know,' Bill said. 'Because your young lady vouched for you.'

She was absolutely not his young lady. No way was Brandon Stone ever going to kiss her again, let alone anything else. But Angel would prefer to have this particular fight in private.

Once Brandon had wrapped up the terms of the deal—and Angel had insisted on washing up the tea things—they left the farmhouse.

As soon as they were out of sight of the farmhouse, Angel said, 'I don't appreciate being used.'

'Used?'

Was he going to deny what he'd done? Angel felt her temper snap. 'You told me about this car, but you said the owner wouldn't sell to you. Clearly you worked out that family and history mean a lot more to him than money, and that's why you brought me along. As leverage. And I don't appreciate it.'

'Actually, I didn't use you.'

She scoffed. 'Come off it.'

'Bill told me he wouldn't sell the car, and I'd pretty much given up trying to persuade him. But I wanted to see the car for myself anyway, and I thought you might like to see it, too—considering that your grandfather built it with mine.'

Which was true. Part of her had been thrilled to see a piece of their joint family history, something from happier times. But she also knew that Brandon was competitive and he liked to win. He'd use every business advantage he could get. 'So are you saying you *didn't* use me to get him to change his mind?'

'No. If I'd thought that strategy would work, I would've contacted you months ago, when I first started talking to Bill, and I would've discussed it with you first.' His mouth thinned. 'Actually, I'm pretty upset that you think I'd be so underhand. I thought we'd got past our family rift and all the nonsense the press writes about me, and we were actually getting to know each other for who we are, not who we thought each other might be.'

His words made Angel feel guilty, but she still couldn't get rid of the suspicion. Not knowing how to deal with the situation, she lapsed into silence. He was clearly just as angry, because he didn't try to make conversation all the way to Keswick.

But when he parked outside the hotel, he turned to her. 'I really wasn't using you today, Angel. We're in separate rooms, so technically we can ignore each other for the rest of today—but then we're going to have a really horrible drive home tomorrow.' He folded his arms. 'I don't want to fight with you. And I'm sorry for not being honest with you right from the start. You told me you didn't like surprises and I didn't listen to you. I thought I was being so clever. I should've just told you that Bill owned one of the first McKenzie-Stone cars and I wanted to see it, and I wanted to share it with you because I thought you'd like to see it as well.'

His eyes were utterly sincere, and guilt flooded through her. Maybe she'd got it wrong after all. And if he'd told her in advance what they were going to see, she would've been really pleased that he'd asked her to go with him. She took a deep breath. 'Then I'm sorry for jumping to conclusions—and for judging you without listening to what you had to say first.'

'Apology accepted,' he said.

'I accept your apology, too.'

'So we're good?'

'We're good,' she confirmed. 'Though I still kind of want to smack you for making me feel used.'

'It sounds to me as if I'd be taking the smack for someone else,' he said. 'Who hurt you, Angel?'

'Nobody.'

He looked as if he didn't believe her; but how could she explain without telling him the shameful truth about her past? The college students who'd seen her as the ice maiden, a challenge to boast about. She couldn't remember their names or their faces now, but she still remembered the hurt when she'd realised they weren't interested in her: they were only interested in boosting their egos and their reputations by being the one who conquered the girl who said no.

To her relief, he dropped the subject and they booked into the hotel. He'd been true to his word and booked them separate rooms. She'd just finished unpacking when there was a knock at her door. Brandon stood in the corridor. 'I, um, was wondering if you might like to go for a walk. Considering we're about ten minutes away from the Derwent and the weather's good.'

And he had pretty much told her about this bit of the weekend in advance, asking her to bring walking shoes.

Guessing that this was a kind of peace offering, she nodded. 'I'll just change my shoes.'

'Come and get me when you're ready,' he said.

She felt awkward, knocking on his door.

'Have you forgiven me yet?' he asked when he opened the door. 'Because I really didn't do anything wrong.'

'I guess.'

She walked alongside him towards the lake, and eventually his hand brushed against hers. Once, twice. She let her hand brush against his. And then finally he linked her fingers with his. Neither of them said anything, and walking in silence among such beautiful scenery eventually lifted her mood.

'It's lovely out here. I haven't been to the Lakes since I was small.'

'Me, neither,' he said. 'We took a boat out. Not here—I can't quite remember where. I was desperate to help row the boat, but I wasn't strong enough. Then Dad sat me on his knee and suddenly I could move the oar.' He smiled. 'Dad was doing all the work, but he let me think I could do it.'

'You're close to your parents?' she asked.

'Yes. That's why I don't race any more. Dad hid it better than Mum, but I know how much he worried. When he had that heart attack and I thought I was going to lose him as well as Sammy, only a couple of weeks apart...' He shuddered. 'Thankfully he recovered. They're both doing OK now.'

'I'm glad.' She tightened her fingers round his. 'And I meant what I said to Bill Edwards. You'll do right by his car.'

'It'll be in pride of place at the museum,' he said. 'What about you?'

'Me?'

'You're close to your parents?'

She nodded. 'I see them or speak to them most days, though they're on an extended tour of Europe at the moment, seeing all the places they've always wanted to see but didn't have time because Dad was so busy at the factory. Mum sent me a selfie of them at the Colosseum yesterday.'

He smiled. 'My mum hasn't quite got the hang of selfies. And the family dog's not very co-operative when she tries to take his picture.'

She smiled back. 'Bill's dog liked you.'

'I like dogs,' he said. 'I've been thinking about getting one. But I'm away on business a lot, so it wouldn't be fair.'

'I can imagine you punting with a spaniel sitting patiently on the deck.'

'Yeah. I'd enjoy that.'

And all of a sudden she had the weirdest picture in her head. Brandon standing on the platform of a punt, the dog sitting on the deck, and herself on the red velvet seat—accompanied by a little boy who was the spitting image of Brandon and desperate to help his father propel the punt along the river, and a baby cradled on her lap.

Where on earth had that come from?

She'd been so focused on the business that she hadn't really thought about her future relationships. She'd never really been one for fantasising about weddings, even when she was small and playing with her cousins. So why was she thinking about it now? And why Brandon?

It spooked her slightly, but she couldn't make the picture in her head go away.

'Everything OK?' he asked.

'Sure.' She gave him her brightest smile, not wanting to admit to what she'd been thinking about.

They stayed by the lake long enough for dusk to fall, then headed back to the hotel for dinner.

'You know what Bill was saying, about the first new McKenzie-Stone car in decades… We could do that,' he said. 'The one you sketched for me.'

'That was just a sketch,' she said. 'It's very different from a full design spec.'

'I know.' He paused. 'You've already said no to my job offer, so I'm not going to ask you again. But maybe we could do this one thing together. You design it, I make it, and it goes out under our joint name.'

It was so very, very tempting.

But they were going to have to heal the rift between their families first. 'We'll see,' she prevaricated.

'Isn't that what people say when they don't want to come straight out with a no?' he asked wryly.

'It'd be a big project. A couple of years, maybe, from the initial thoughts to final production. I'm not sure either of us could fit it in.'

'We could make the time.'

'Maybe.'

'So what's your big ambition?' he asked.

'For McKenzie's or for me?'

'Both.'

'I guess it's the same thing,' she said. 'I want to design the iconic car for my generation. Granddad made the Mermaid, Dad made the Luna, and I...' She stopped, realising how close she'd come to telling him about the Frost.

'You,' he said, 'will make something amazing, because your ideas are great.'

Should she tell him?

But they were still business rivals. And the Frost was still under wraps. Better to say nothing for now. Though it warmed her that he actually seemed to believe in her.

After dinner, they sat in the hotel's garden and watched the stars come out. As the night air began to cool, she shivered.

'Cold?'

'A bit,' she admitted.

He slid his arm round her shoulders. 'Better?'

'A little.'

'That was a polite fib,' he said. 'Let's go inside.'

But he didn't take his arm away as they walked back into the hotel.

Outside the door to her room, he said, 'Come and sit with me for a while.'

Her mouth went dry.

'Just sit with me,' he said. 'I'm not going to push you into anything you don't want.'

She believed him. The problem was, she was starting to want more. 'OK.'

'Your choice,' he said as he unlocked the door. 'Chair or bed?' He paused. 'Or we could both sit in the chair.'

'Both?'

'Like this.' He scooped her up, sat down and settled her in his lap.

To keep her balance, she slid her arms round his neck.

'You know what you said to me about hating myself being pointless because it won't bring Sam back?'

She winced. 'Sorry. That was a bit harsh.'

'Don't apologise. It was something I needed to hear.' He leaned his forehead against hers. 'It's true about the car, too.'

'The car?' She didn't quite understand.

'It was Sammy's dream to complete the museum collection,' he said. 'So when this opportunity came up... It's why I wanted to buy the car. For Sammy.'

'And it doesn't make any difference?' she asked softly.

'It doesn't make any difference,' he confirmed. 'The hole in the centre of my world's still there.'

She stroked his face. 'I'm sorry. But I bet he's proud of you.'

'What, for haranguing an old man for months?' He lifted one shoulder in a half-shrug.

'If you'd told Bill Edwards why you wanted the car so much, he probably would've sold it to you months ago.'

He frowned. 'Why?'

'Because you weren't doing it for you, you were doing it for Sam. Meaning you're not one of the ruthless Stones.'

'Ruthless?' He stared at her for a moment, then sighed. 'OK. I guess you have a point. After your grandmother broke my grandfather's heart, apparently he was pretty focused on the business.'

'But he must've fallen in love with someone else, or you wouldn't be here,' she pointed out.

'I guess.' He paused. 'I didn't really know Barnaby. He died when I was too young to remember him. But Dad was always pretty focused on the business, too.' He grimaced. 'I know he tried to buy McKenzie's in the last recession.'

'That kind of explains why my dad always muttered about your family being ruthless,' she said thoughtfully.

'He sold his entire private collection of cars to make sure he didn't have to sell McKenzie's.'

'A whole collection at short notice?' Brandon grimaced. 'The sharks would've circled and he would've got less than it was worth.'

'It was enough to keep the bank happy,' she said dryly. 'So is that why you want to buy McKenzie's now? For your dad, or for Sam?'

'Maybe,' Brandon said. 'I don't know if Sam would've wanted to buy you out or not. We never discussed it.' He sighed. 'You're right. Sam was the best of us, but nearly all the Stone men are ruthless. Dad was—until Sammy died. It changed him.'

She could believe that. But Brandon... Brandon was different. 'I'm not so sure that you're ruthless,' she said.

He shook his head. 'I always went out on the track with the aim of being first past the finishing line. There have been times when I could've let someone win a race. When maybe I should've let them win, because I knew they'd been having a hard time; winning a race might've helped them turn things around.'

'And what if they'd found out the truth later—that their own skill and efforts weren't really enough to let them win? It would've punched a hole right through their victory and probably made them feel worse than if they'd come second,' she pointed out. 'Anyway, if you were really ruthless, you would've replaced Gina ages ago with someone younger and with longer legs.'

He scoffed. 'Gina's an excellent secretary. I don't need to replace her.'

'She's a bit more than that,' Angel said. 'She mothers you.'

He raised an eyebrow. 'I can hardly sack my mum's best friend. Particularly as she does a good job.'

'I think you like having her around.'

'Gina's been good to me,' he said softly. 'She's the only one at the factory who believed I could do it when I took over from Dad.'

That truly shocked her. 'Didn't your parents believe in you?'

'Sammy's death broke them.' He looked away. 'I don't think they could believe in anything, right then. So I had to step up to the plate. I couldn't let my family down.'

'Even though Sammy's death broke you, too?' she asked softly.

'I thought working until I was practically comatose from tiredness would get me through it. It kind of did. That and burning the candle the other end and still doing all the racing driver social stuff. But I still don't know how to make the empty spaces go away,' he said, his grey eyes filled with sadness. 'Nothing works.'

She didn't know how to make him feel better, but she had to try. There was only one thing she could think of that might fill the empty spaces.

It was a risk.

A huge risk.

But one she was prepared to take. She leaned forward and kissed him.

His eyes went very dark. 'Angel, my self-control's pretty good, but it's not perfect.'

She felt the colour flood through her cheeks. 'Sorry.'

He stole a kiss. 'Don't apologise.' Then he sighed and traced her lower lip with the pad of his thumb. 'Maybe this is a bad idea. Maybe I should just see you back to your room.'

'Or maybe,' she said, 'this is a good idea.'

His eyes widened. 'Are you suggesting…?'

For a moment, she couldn't breathe. This might be the

most monumentally stupid thing she'd ever done. Or it might be the best idea she'd ever had.

There was only one way to find out.

'Yes. Make love with me, Brandon,' she whispered.

She could feel the tension in his body. 'Are you sure about this?'

Not entirely. But she was tired of being a coward. 'Yes.'

CHAPTER NINE

AFTERWARDS, BRANDON LAY with Angel curled in his arms.

And he was absolutely terrified.

He'd always kept emotional distance between himself and his girlfriends. Always. But he'd let Angel closer than he'd ever let anyone in his life. Told her things he never even discussed with his closest family. He hadn't even sat at Sammy's grave and spilled this kind of stuff, and his brother's grave was the place where he went to spill things. When nobody could hear.

What made him even antsier was that, at the same time, he felt at peace with the world. And it wasn't just the sweet relaxation he usually felt after sex. This was something different. As if something had shifted inside him. As if the empty spaces weren't empty any more.

Was he falling in love with Angel McKenzie?

And what was he going to do about it? Particularly as there was something he and Angel really had to discuss.

OK. Time for a reality check. 'Angel,' he said, stroking her hair. 'We need to talk.'

'Uh-huh.' There was a pause, and then her voice sounded all super-bright. 'Is this where you tell me this was a mistake, it's your fault and not mine, and I need to go back to my own room?'

She hadn't pulled her punches. He dragged in a breath. 'No. Do you really think I'm that cold?'

Her silence confirmed his worst fears.

He sighed. 'The press has a lot to answer for. That's not who I… Well, I admit, I have done that in the past, and it wasn't very gallant of me. But I don't want you to go.'

'So what do you want to talk about?'

'The elephant in the room.'

'What elephant?'

He stole another kiss. 'OK. If you want me to be the one to say it. You just gave me your virginity.'

She blushed. He'd never seen anyone go so red before. 'It's so ridiculous, being a virgin at the age of thirty in this day and age.'

'No, it means…' That it was important to her. And he felt incredibly guilty. How could he explain that without making her feel awkward?

She bit her lip and looked away. 'I'm just not good at relationships. I was too shy to date anyone at school, then somehow everyone at university thought of me as an ice maiden, and I didn't want to be just a challenge that people boasted about conquering.'

'That,' he said, 'shows incredible strength of character. You didn't let anyone push you into doing anything you didn't want to do.'

'So you don't think I'm—well—pathetic? Or there's something wrong with me?'

'What?' He stared at her in utter shock. 'You're kidding. You're not pathetic in the slightest and there's nothing wrong with you.' He dragged in a breath. 'I feel honoured, actually. That you trusted me. And I feel guilty, because if you were saving—'

'—myself for my wedding night?' She cut in. 'I wasn't. And I wasn't using you to get rid of my virginity, either.

I… I could see you were hurting, and I wanted to make you feel better, and…'

'One thing led to another,' he finished.

She lifted her chin. 'I don't regret it, so don't feel guilty.'

'I don't regret it, either.' He stroked her face. 'I talk too much.'

'Agreed. Sometimes it's easier to sweep things under the carpet, but you don't do things the easy way, do you?'

'I probably do. That's why Eric calls me Golden Boy.'

'Eric's bitter,' she said. 'And wasn't King Midas—the original golden boy—lonely, when all he had was gold?'

'You scare me,' he said, 'because you see things that other people miss.'

'Comes of lip-reading,' she said lightly.

'Stay with me tonight,' he said, surprising himself.

'Is this a good idea?'

'Probably not,' he admitted. 'But I don't want you to go.'

'I don't want to go, either,' she said.

'Then let's stop talking and just go to sleep.'

She chuckled.

'What's so funny?' he asked.

'You're the one who said we needed to talk.'

'Sometimes,' he said, 'I'm wrong.'

She laughed. 'I'm glad you can admit that.'

'Me, too.' He kissed her.

He reached over to turn off the bedside light, then moved so that his body was curled round hers and his arm was wrapped round her waist, holding her close against him. Her breathing slowed and she relaxed back against him as she fell asleep, but Brandon stayed awake for longer. This was the first time in years that he'd actually shared a bed with someone and it didn't involve just sex. Why had he asked her to stay? Guilt, because he'd taken her virginity? Or was it that her obvious trust in him had made him relax enough to trust her with himself?

He couldn't quite work out how he felt about Angel McKenzie. What he did know was that she'd changed him. She made him feel as if maybe he had a soft centre after all, instead of a heart of granite wrapped around an empty space. He wasn't sure if that was a good thing or a bad, but for now he'd go with it.

The next morning, Brandon woke first and kissed Angel awake. He was rewarded with confusion in those beautiful violet eyes clearing, and then she gave him a smile of pure unadulterated warmth, as if she was glad to be waking in his arms. Weird that it suddenly made him feel as if he were ten feet tall.

'Good morning,' he said softly.

She stroked his face. 'Good morning.'

'Did you sleep OK?'

'Yes.'

'Good.' He couldn't resist stealing another kiss. 'Do you have to be back home as soon as possible?'

'Do you?'

'No. And as we're in one of the most romantic places in England, I thought it might be nice to go for a walk— oh, and holding my hand is obligatory.'

'Are you always this bossy?' she asked, but her eyes were lit with amusement.

'Pretty much.' He grinned. 'So are you, so this is going to be interesting.'

She bit her lip. 'About last night...'

'I stand by what I said,' he said softly. 'I don't regret a second of it. And I still feel really honoured that you trusted me that much.'

He saw her eyes fill with tears, even though she blinked them away immediately.

'Don't cry,' he said. 'Or was it that bad?'

'No, it was…' She paused, as if not knowing what to say.

'If you tell me I'm like your favourite engine…' he teased.

She laughed. 'Ah, but aren't you meant to do nought to top speed more slowly in this sort of thing?'

He liked the fact that she could laugh at herself, even though he knew she'd felt awkward about her inexperience. He held her close, laughing, and kissed the top of her head. 'Let's have a shower and breakfast, and go for that walk.'

Over breakfast, they pored over his phone and discovered that one of the prettiest sights in the Lakes was only a short drive away. The road, being a narrow single track, was busy and they had to wait at several passing places, but finally they were able to park by Wastwater.

'Oh, now that's definitely worth the wait,' Angel said, gesturing to the way the mountains reflected in the water. 'I can see why it's listed as one of the best views.'

'The deepest lake in England,' he said, referring to a page on his phone. 'And that bit over there is Scafell Pike, England's highest mountain.'

'Don't tell me—you've climbed it?' she asked.

He smiled. 'No. And I don't think we have time to do it today. But maybe we could come back, if you want to climb it?'

'I'm happy just to look at it and admire it,' she said, smiling back.

'OK.' He paused. 'Can we…?' He waved his phone at her.

'Selfie? Sure.'

He took a quick snap of them together. Again, it was

weird: he never did this sort of things with his girlfriends. But with Angel, it felt right.

'Send it to me, please?' she asked.

'Sure.' This was definitely starting to feel official. Even six months ago, that feeling would've sent him running as fast as possible in the opposite direction. But he was actually enjoying this.

He enjoyed the drive back to Cambridge even more, because Angel seemed so much more relaxed with him. This time, he shared the driving with her, and it was so good to talk to her about the car and discuss its pros and cons. Particularly as Angel was talking from an engineer's viewpoint, giving him a completely different perspective.

And he enjoyed the fact that she was comfortable with him looking through the music on her phone and choosing what to play. 'This is really retro stuff,' he said. 'Half of this would go better with the Mermaid.'

'If that's an offer...' she teased.

He grinned. 'Oh, it is. If we pick a time when the weather's good, we can have the roof down and drive along the nearest coast.'

'Oxford's pretty much smack in the middle of the country,' she said. 'And Cambridge is a good ninety minutes from the coast. You'd be looking at Norfolk or Suffolk.'

'Fish and chips, ice cream and candy floss,' he said promptly. 'It's a deal.'

She laughed. 'And a kiss-me-quick hat?'

'I'd prefer you to kiss me slowly,' he said. 'But the coast would be fun.'

'I'd like that,' she said.

'Then it's a date. An open-ended one because it's weather-dependent, but a definite date,' he said. And how weird it felt to be planning things in the future with her. Normally he didn't let people that close. But Angel...

Angel was different. She made him want to do this kind of thing.

When they arrived in Cambridge, she turned to him. 'I would offer to cook you dinner before you go back to Oxford, but, um…'

'You have work to do?'

'It's much more shameful than that,' she said. 'I have an empty fridge. And I'm not much of a cook anyway. I normally get in a stack of ready meals from the supermarket to keep me going during the week, but I forgot to go shopping on Friday night.'

'Well, I'm not leaving you here with an empty fridge,' he said. 'The supermarkets are all closed by now, so either we find a nice little pub somewhere or we get a takeaway.'

'Either's fine.' She paused. 'I've got milk.'

'Milk?' He wasn't quite following her line of thought.

'I normally have a protein shake for breakfast before the gym,' she said. 'But the baker round the corner opens really early in the morning. They do the best croissants in Cambridge.'

He caught his breath. 'Are you asking me to stay for breakfast?'

'Inviting you, yes.' She gave him the shyest, cutest smile. 'If you want to.'

Oh, he wanted to. He smiled. 'Provided you let me do the washing up.'

'I thought you said you had troglodyte tendencies?'

'I'm domesticated. To a point.' Though it spooked him slightly how domesticated he wanted to be with her. He could imagine waking up with her on Sunday mornings, lazing in bed with coffee and the papers and a bacon sandwich.

Her little Victorian terraced house turned out to be totally what he'd expected: neat, with everything in its place. There were family photographs everywhere, and arty black and white prints of close-up details from classic cars. And it felt way more like home than his own, much larger house. Personal. Full of warmth.

Then again, it was his own fault for using an interior designer instead of spending the time to make his house feel like a personal space.

Just as she'd promised, the croissants at breakfast were superb. And leaving her after he'd insisted on doing the washing up after breakfast turned out to be a real wrench. He actually missed her all the way to Oxford, and the only time the ache went was when he threw himself into work.

A few unexpected glitches meant that he didn't have time to meet up with Angel during the week, even if they'd driven to a halfway point. And he was shocked by how much he missed her and wanted to be with her.

Dating her had been supposed to be a way of getting her out of his system and persuading her to sell McKenzie's to him, but it hadn't worked out that way. If anything, he wanted to spend more time with her. The sensible side of him knew that he ought to back off right now, before he got in too deeply.

But then he found himself video-calling her.

'Hey,' she said, and smiled at him.

Oh, man. He'd never understood before when people said that someone made their heart flip. Now he did. Angel's smile did exactly that. 'How are you doing?' he asked.

She laughed. 'Say that for me again, but this time in a Joey Tribbiani voice.'

'*Friends* fan, hmm?'

'Joey's the best. Indulge me.'

He grinned and did what she asked.

'Be still, my beating heart.' She fanned herself.

Brandon almost told her how cute she looked, but stopped himself just in time.

'So how are things?' she asked.

'Wall-to-wall meetings.' Some of them with staff who'd had a spat with Eric and needed their feathers unruffled, which drove him crazy. 'How about you?'

'Similar.'

He wasn't going to tell her he missed her.

He *wasn't*.

'Can I see you at the weekend?' He cringed inwardly as the words came out of his mouth. How needy was that?

But she went pink. 'OK.'

'Come to me?' he suggested. 'If you stay overnight Saturday, I'll cook dinner for you.'

'You cook?' She looked surprised. And then she gave him the cheekiest grin. 'Wait. I forgot. You're good at *everything.*'

The breathy little way she said that sent desire lancing straight through him. 'Nearly,' he said. Right now he didn't seem to be very good at keeping his feelings under control. And his voice had gone all husky. He really hoped she hadn't noticed—or, if she had, that she hadn't guessed why.

'I'll be with you at nine,' she promised. 'Send me your postcode for my satnav.'

'I will.' He stopped himself telling her that he missed her. 'See you on Saturday.'

'How does it go?' She wrinkled her nose at him. 'Ah, yes. *Ciao.*'

No. Just no. He was *not* supposed to find it super-cute that she was teasing him about the ridiculously corny way he'd once said goodbye to her. Or want to drop everything and drive for two hours plus whatever hold-ups he encountered on the motorway just to kiss her goodnight.

'Ciao,' he drawled, and cut the connection.

* * *

On Saturday morning, Angel drove to Oxford, tingling with anticipation. Would Brandon have changed his mind about their relationship by the time she got there? Because she was pretty sure the women he reportedly saw only lasted three dates, and they'd already gone beyond that. Was he even now rehearsing a speech? *It's not you, it's me...*

But all her doubts melted when she parked on the gravel outside his unexpectedly large house and he walked out of the front door to greet her. The warmth of his kiss told her that he hadn't been rehearsing any speeches at all—and that he'd missed her as much as she'd missed him.

Not that she was going to bring that up. Brandon Stone wasn't the kind of man who liked talking about emotions, and she didn't want to make things awkward between them. And she definitely wasn't going to tell him that she was falling for him. She knew it'd make him run a mile.

'Hey.' She stole another kiss. 'Flashy house, Mr Stone. Are you sure you're not a secret rock star?'

He laughed. 'No. You'll probably find the garage more interesting than the house.'

'Garage? That looks more like an aircraft hangar,' she teased.

'Yeah, yeah.' But he grinned and held her close.

'So do I get to see your collection?'

'Later,' he said. 'And I'm not fobbing you off—I'm looking forward to showing you.' He stole another kiss. 'It's your fault you have to wait.'

'How?' she asked.

'Because,' he said, 'you've given me back the joy I used to find in racing cars. I lost it for a while.'

Since his brother's death, she guessed.

'One of the local stately homes is having an open

day—usually they're not open to the public, but today it's a charity thing to show off their garden. And there just so happens to be a vintage car rally in their deer park. I thought you might like to go.'

'Great idea. I take it we're going in the Mermaid?'

'We are. Want to drive?'

'Stupid question,' she said, and kissed him.

Once he'd taken her bag inside and locked up the house, he handed her the car keys. 'I'll direct you,' he said.

Angel thoroughly enjoyed driving the car—and she enjoyed being with Brandon even more. The stately home's garden turned out to be amazing, full of cottage garden plants with butterflies and bees everywhere and a secret garden full of roses. She loved wandering round, hand in hand with Brandon—particularly when he managed to find several hidden alcoves where he could steal a kiss in private.

The vintage car rally was fabulous, too, and they had a wonderful time arguing over the merits of their favourites and trying to convince each other to change their mind.

'You know, the red car on the end there,' Brandon said, 'has been used in a film.'

Cars and films. Angel went cold for a moment. Was this his way of telling her that he knew about Triffid and the Frost? Triffid's PR team had put her in touch with several magazines for features, but they'd all been thoroughly screened and there was an embargo in place. Then again, no matter how careful you were, there were always leaks. News like that would filter through pretty quickly to fellow car manufacturers. Maybe that was how he knew.

But then he turned the conversation to something else, and it didn't feel like quite the right time to tell him about why she didn't need to sell McKenzie's to him.

Back at his house, Brandon proved that his flashy

kitchen wasn't all for show. He produced grilled bream, crushed new potatoes with mint and butter, and steamed asparagus and samphire, all beautifully presented.

'That was utterly gorgeous,' she said when she'd finished. 'If I hadn't been sitting at your kitchen table and seen you cooking this from scratch, I would've guessed that you'd hired a caterer.'

'I did cheat by buying the cheesecake,' he admitted. 'I'm rubbish at puddings.'

'Tsk—and I thought you were good at everything,' she teased.

'Just for that,' he said, 'you can wait for your pudding until you agree that I am.' And he hauled her over his shoulder and carried her off to his bed.

Back in Cambridge, Angel called her parents. 'Hey. So how's Florence?' she asked.

'Wonderful. Is everything OK with you?' Max asked.

'Yes. And you don't need to worry about the business. Everything's fine.'

'Of course it is, with my girl in charge.' She could practically hear the smile in her father's voice. 'But you sound a bit worried.'

'I, um… This might be a bit of a Romeo and Juliet moment.'

'We're in Florence, not Verona,' her father teased.

'I'm, um, seeing someone.' She swallowed hard. 'Brandon Stone.'

'Larry Stone's son?' Max asked, sounding shocked.

'Is it a problem for you, Dad?'

He blew out a breath. 'Actually, love, it is. The Stones are a ruthless bunch. I remember Mum saying once that she chose Dad over Barnaby, because Dad was kind and

Barnaby was driven. Barnaby's sons and his grandsons are chips off the old block—and I don't want you to get hurt.'

'I'm thirty, Dad.'

'I know. But you're my daughter, and I worry about you. If you really have to date the guy, date him. But be careful.' He paused. 'And if he hurts you, he'll have me to deal with.'

'Dad, it's not going to be like that. But thank you for— well, doing what dads do.'

'I meant it,' Max said softly. 'If he hurts you…'

'He won't. He's actually a decent guy.'

'Who's photographed with a different woman on his arm every week.'

'That's the press blowing stuff out of proportion, Dad,' she said softly.

Max sighed. 'All right. You're old enough to know what you're doing. But please be careful,' he said again.

She didn't exactly have her father's blessing, but she didn't quite have his opposition, either, Angel thought. He might have a point about her needing to be careful. She liked spending time with Brandon, but their families were at loggerheads. And Brandon himself had told her that he was about to start developing cars that would be in direct competition with hers. He could afford to drop his prices enough to undercut hers and torpedo her sales.

But she didn't think he'd do that. Brandon had integrity. She'd trusted him with herself, and he hadn't let her down. So could she trust him enough to talk to him about her business—to share the new design with him? It was a risk: it would mean breaking confidentiality, giving him what could be a business advantage. But he wasn't the ruthless, selfish playboy she'd originally thought he was. He had a heart—one that had been broken—and he kept people at a distance to protect himself. Yet he'd trusted her enough to let her close. Maybe she should do the same. She thought about it all week.

And thought about it some more over the next weekend, when Brandon swept her off to the coast in the Mermaid so they could walk hand in hand by the edge of the sea.

The way she felt when she was with him—it was like nothing else she'd ever experienced.

Love?

Maybe. But she'd spent so long struggling on her own, trying to keep everything together and yet unable to talk to her parents about the problems because she was trying to protect them and let them enjoy their retirement. Just for once it would be good to lean on someone, share her worries—and share the joy, too.

He'd said she'd given him back the joy he'd once found in cars. And she'd really value his opinion of the Frost. Maybe it was time to trust him back.

'Can we call in to the factory?' she asked on the way back to her house.

'Sure. Is there something you need to do for work?'

'No. There's something I want to show you.'

He gave her a sidelong look. 'Such as?'

'You'll see when we get there.'

'Should I be worried?'

She smiled. 'No.' But her own fears were back. Was she taking too much of a risk?

As if he guessed that she was warring with herself mentally, he didn't push her to talk further until they got to the factory and she took him into the partitioned-off area.

'This is confidential,' she warned. 'Strictly confidential.'

'Got it. So what did you want to show me?'

'This,' she said, and whisked the tarpaulin off her prototype.

'Oh.' He prowled round it, clearly analysing it and inspecting every little detail. And then he straightened up. 'I'm assuming the design is all yours?'

'And I helped put it together. The engine's all mine,' she said.

'It's *stunning*,' he said. 'May I?' His hand hovered above the bonnet.

She nodded, and he ran his fingers lightly over the paintwork. 'I love the lines of it. And I've never seen a colour like this. Did you use one of your granddad's paint techniques—something from the Mermaid years?'

'No. I wanted the car to be shimmery, like the Mermaid, but I wanted the effect to be otherworldly rather than undersea,' she said. 'It's plain ivory paint.'

'No way is that just ivory,' he said.

'With a little bit of silver pearlescence—I wanted it to be like the moonlight glittering on grass on a winter night.' She paused. 'It's called the McKenzie Frost.'

'And that colour's perfect for the name.' He indicated the door. 'Can I sit in it?'

'Sure.'

He climbed inside, and again there was silence while he looked at the interior.

And then he leaned over and opened the passenger door.

'I want one,' he said simply.

Then she realised how tense her muscles had been while she'd waited for his verdict. 'You like it?'

'More than like it,' he corrected. 'And I want one in my private collection.'

'Technically, it doesn't exist. This is the prototype. It's had a couple of photo shoots, but the world hasn't seen it yet,' she warned.

'Then put me at the head of your pre-order list because I mean it—I really, really want one. And I don't care how much it costs.'

She smiled. 'Are you telling me to overcharge you?'

'No. I'm telling you I want the first production model and I'm prepared to pay a premium for it.'

He was serious. She could see it in his eyes. And it made her heart sing. 'I can't do that, I'm afraid. The first five are already taken.'

'I thought you said you didn't have a pre-order list?'

'I designed this for a specific customer,' she said. 'Triffid Studios.'

'The movie company?'

She nodded. 'It's going to be in the next *Spyline* movie. The deal is they have exclusive use until next summer. But I'll be taking pre-orders when it's announced formally, in about six weeks.'

'I see why you said it's confidential.' He paused. 'And you trust me?'

'Considering our family history, I ought to say no,' she admitted. 'But, yes. I trust you.' The man she'd got to know over the last few weeks was honourable and decent.

'Thank you. I'll respect your confidentiality.' He ran his hands over the steering wheel. 'You know you said you wanted to produce the iconic design of our generation?'

'Uh-huh.'

'I thought it might be the car you started sketching in the tea shop.' *Their* car. 'But you've already done it with this.'

She felt her eyes film with tears. He really thought that highly of her design? 'You're not just flattering me?'

'I'm never more serious than when I'm talking about cars,' he said, and rubbed the steering wheel again. 'I probably shouldn't ask this, and I promise I'm not pressuring you… But I'm dying to know how it handles. Can I drive it?'

'It's a prototype, so it's not perfect,' she warned. 'There are a few things I want to iron out for when it goes into production.'

'Noted, and I'll keep the speed low,' he promised. 'Come with me?'

'Sure. I'll open the doors and you can take it round the track.'

As he'd promised, Brandon drove the Frost carefully, then returned it equally carefully through the hangar doors into its spot in the factory.

'I love the design,' he said. 'But you're right—there are a couple of things that need ironing out, and I think it could be improved from a driving point of view.'

'Tell me.'

He began to list them, and Angel said, 'Hang on a tick.' She grabbed her phone and tapped into the notes section. 'OK. Start again, please.'

He nodded, and went through his thoughts.

'Thank you,' she said when he'd finished. 'I did this as speech to text and it sometimes gets things wrong, so can I send you the text file to review?'

'Of course you can. And if I think of anything else I'll add it to the list.' He raised an eyebrow. 'Our grandfathers would never believe it. A McKenzie listening to a Stone.'

'An engineer listening to a professional driver,' she corrected.

'The same as when you started sketching the car I was talking about and pointed out the aerodynamic issues— that was a driver listening to an engineer.'

'No, it was a Stone listening to a McKenzie,' she teased.

He laughed. 'This is just you and me—and thank you so much for sharing this with me. It's amazing.'

'It's the reason why I don't have to sell the company,' she said. 'I couldn't tell you before. But I'm sorry. McKenzie's really isn't for sale.'

'I understand.' He looked sad. 'And with you putting this in production, you're really not going to have time to do some freelance stuff and work with me on our joint car. That's a pity, because I really would've liked working with you.'

'And I with you,' she said, 'Though I don't think I could work with your uncle.'

'Not many people can,' he said with a grimace, 'but I'm going to have to put up with him until he decides he wants to retire. He's too old to change the way he acts in business, and I'm not going to humiliate him by making him jump before he's pushed. But, just so you know, I wouldn't have let him anywhere near your team if I'd bought you out.'

'I'm glad to hear it,' she said dryly. 'And I'm also glad you don't have to buy me out.'

'The Frost,' he said, 'is beautiful. You're amazing. I'm so proud of you.' His grey eyes were completely sincere, and Angel's heart felt as if it had performed a somersault. 'And I mean it about wanting one when it goes into production properly. I want to be top of your list.'

'You've got it,' she said softly. And she was starting to think that he was top of her list in a lot of other ways, too. If she wasn't careful, she could lose her heart to Brandon Stone.

But would that be such a bad thing?

When Brandon drove back to Oxford on Sunday evening, he made a slight detour via the churchyard in the village. He didn't bother taking flowers, because he knew that between them his mother and Maria always had that covered, but he sat down in front of his brother's grave.

'Hey, Sammy,' he said softly. 'My original Plan A isn't going to work, because McKenzie's isn't for sale. But I think I might just have something even better.' He smiled. 'It's all about a girl. But this one's special. I really like her, Sammy, and I think she might like me back.' In a way he'd never expected, and never experienced before. 'Remember when I used to tease you about being all soppy over Maria? I think I could be like that about Angel McKenzie. No, actually, I think I already might be. Dating her was supposed to get her out of my system, but it's done nothing of the kind. I wanted to charm her into selling to me—but now I just want her to be with me.'

And he could really do with a bit of advice from his brother right now. Not that he'd get it. But he could at least talk to Sam, even if Sam couldn't talk back.

'You're the one person I could talk to about this,' he said. 'I think I might actually be in love. For the first time ever. And it makes me feel as if I don't have a clue what I'm doing. I've always been in control and I've always been able to walk away. But Angel… She's different. I want to be with her. I want to end this stupid feud between our family and hers, and I want a future with her smack in the centre of it.' He gave a wry smile.

'I can't imagine getting married without you as my best man. But until I met Angel I couldn't imagine getting married at all. I haven't asked her. She might even say no. But I think finally I know who I want to be, thanks to her. It's as if I've found my way back out of a black hole. And I'm a better man when I'm with her.' There was just one sticking point. 'Let's just hope we can talk the Montagues and Capulets round.'

CHAPTER TEN

ON FRIDAY AFTERNOON, Brandon arrived to drive Angel to London for the ball. He kept the conversation light, but Angel felt her nervousness growing as they neared the city.

The hotel was seriously posh: it actually had a doorman who wore a top hat and tails. Inside, there was an amazing marble staircase, and all the decor was rich greens and golds.

Parties were the things she hated most. Where people made small talk and she couldn't always pick it up because there was so much background noise and the lighting wasn't good enough to let her lip-read. Conferences, presentations, lectures and interviews were fine. Parties were the seventh circle of hell; if she couldn't fall back on her usual strategy of talking cars, she knew she'd struggle.

Brandon had clearly guessed what was worrying her, because he paused outside the door to her room. 'We don't have to do this, you know,' he said. 'We can skip it and do something else. Go to the theatre. The cinema. Just for a walk along the river. Anything you like.'

'No. You won the bet, and I agreed to go with you. I'm not reneging on that,' she said. 'And people will expect to see you there.'

'I know parties are difficult for you,' he said. 'Look, when you've had enough, let me know and we'll escape.

And I'm staying right by your side tonight—just squeeze my hand or arm twice if you think you've missed something and you need me to rescue you.'

Angel felt close to tears. She really hadn't expected Brandon to be this thoughtful. 'Thanks.'

'Let's get ready,' he said. 'And there's no pressure. Any time you want to leave, we leave.'

'OK.' She took a deep breath. She could be brave about this. She *would* be brave about this.

The room was stunning, with views over the River Thames; she could see the London Eye and the South Bank. Even though the building was very old, the room itself felt completely modern.

She'd just finished changing when he knocked on her door.

His jaw dropped when he saw her. 'Wow. You look stunning.'

Her dress was dark red and A-line, with a skirt that flared out to just below her knees, a sweetheart off-the-shoulder neckline and lacy sleeves that went down to her elbows; she'd teamed it with dark red patent high heels. Angel had spent hours online, trying to find the perfect dress; thankfully, it looked as if it had been worth the effort. 'Thanks. You look pretty amazing, too. The outfit really suited him: a dinner jacket, slim-fitting dark trousers, a crisp white shirt and a black bow tie.

'Sorry—I didn't mean to sound shallow. It's just I've never seen you dressed up like this before.' He smiled. 'I think a lot of people are going to want to dance with you tonight.'

'I hope they're wearing steel-capped shoes, then, or they're going to get bruises.'

He grinned. 'Good.' Then he frowned. 'Hang on, are you telling me you can't dance?'

'I've never really had any cause to,' she admitted.

'All right.' He stood in front of her. 'Let me show you the ballroom hold.' He put her left hand on his right shoulder, and supported her arm with his right arm; then he took her right hand and lifted it up. 'Just follow my lead and it'll be fine.' And, to her surprise, he danced down the corridor with her.

'I feel a bit like Cinderella,' she said.

'My very shy Cinderella.' He stole a kiss. 'Except there aren't going to be any pumpkins at midnight. And you're not going to lose a shoe.'

'I hope not.' She forced herself to smile.

Together they went into the ballroom where the gala dinner was being held. The tables were all laid with snowy white linen and decorated with beautiful arrangements of white flowers; the room itself was incredibly glamorous, with pillars around the edges, floor-to-ceiling windows with heavy velvet drapes, and metalwork chandeliers with delicate glass shades.

And the background noise, particularly when it was amplified by the wooden floor, was horrendous.

'Twice for help,' he said, making sure that she could see his mouth.

Dreading it, she nodded.

Brandon seemed to know just about everyone in the room—well, of course he would, because a lot of them came from the motor racing world. Angel noticed that a lot of the women were staring at them, and a tight knot of nerves formed in her stomach. She wasn't the best at small talk. Hopefully she could get people talking about themselves and it would take the spotlight off her.

She was relieved when Brandon introduced her to a couple of the other drivers, and they started talking about engines and aerodynamics. At least this was a subject she felt comfortable with. And although the other drivers looked surprised at first, they were soon chatting to her as if she was one of them.

Dinner was slightly more difficult, because Angel was placed opposite Brandon rather than next to him. The man sitting on her left had a beard and she really couldn't work out what he was saying, half the time, but she hoped that she was nodding and smiling in all the right places.

Finally it was time for the dancing. Just as Brandon had promised, he stayed with her the whole time, not letting anyone else dance with her. She followed his lead, as he'd directed, and was shocked to find that not only did she feel as if she could dance, she was actually enjoying it. The way he whirled her round the floor made her feel like a princess.

'Midnight,' Brandon said against her ear. 'And not a pumpkin or a glass slipper in sight. Want to stay a bit longer, or do you want to escape?'

'Both,' she admitted. 'I want to dance with you.' And she wanted to be alone with him, too, though it felt a bit pushy to say so.

He laughed. 'One more dance,' he said, and stole a kiss.

And then finally they slipped away together.

'Stay with me tonight?' he asked as they stood outside the doors to their rooms.

How could she resist her very own Prince Charming? She smiled. 'Yes.'

The next morning, Angel woke early. Brandon was sprawled out, still asleep, and she smiled. It was tempting to wake him; but she could really do with a swim and he looked as if he could do with catching up on his sleep.

She managed to climb out of bed without waking him, then scribbled him a quick note and left it on her pillow.

Gone for a swim. See you in the pool or next door.

Then she put on enough clothes to make her decent, tip-toed out of his room, and went next door to her own room to change into her swimming things.

When she dropped her bag on her bed, her phone fell out; she could see that she had several voicemails. She'd kept her phone on silent during the ball and had forgotten to switch the ringer on again afterwards, so she'd clearly missed a call.

Worried that it might be her parents, and something was wrong, she listened to the messages.

But they weren't from her parents.

They were from the legal team at Triffid. Half a dozen of them asking her to call them urgently, and then a longer one which she had to listen to twice before she could make sense of it.

'Miss McKenzie, you should have told us about the takeover. We made the contract with you, not with Stone's. You've also broken the contract terms by breaking the embargo. You've made it clear that the deal's off and we'll have to go with another manufacturer. We may have to look at compensation if it holds up the film.'

Compensation? What? Were they talking about suing her? She stared at her phone in horror. What takeover? And what did they mean about breaking the embargo? Was there something about the Frost in the news?

She flicked into her favourite news site to see if she could find out what had happened and saw the headline straight away: *Racing Champ's Successful Takeover.*

According to the lead paragraph, Brandon Stone was buying McKenzie's. There was a picture of them together from last night, at the ball; she was looking all gooey-eyed at him, and he looked like a predator.

She stared at it, totally shocked. Where had the story come from? The small print talked about 'sources close to the company'; did that mean Brandon himself? Had last night simply been a set-up?

Angel didn't want to believe it. She knew she'd got his motivations completely wrong before, when he'd taken her to Cumbria, and she'd learned from that not to jump to conclusions. Her father had warned her that he was as ruthless as the rest of his family, but the Brandon she'd got to know was one of the good guys. He wouldn't betray her like that.

But the final paragraph was the killer. It talked about the new car. The Frost. It even mentioned the iridescent shimmery ivory paint: a detail that hardly anyone knew. Nobody at McKenzie's would've said a single thing about the Triffid deal: her staff had always been incredibly loyal and they'd worked as hard as she had on the Frost.

She dragged in a breath. The evidence was all in the article. No matter how much she didn't want to believe it, everything pointed to Brandon being the source. And, thanks to his deliberate leak, she'd lost the contract with Triffid. All the work she'd done, the hours she'd put in and the worrying, had been for nothing.

McKenzie's was going to the wall.

He'd ruined her company.

Sick to her stomach, she didn't bother going for a swim. She simply showered, dressed and packed. And then, filled with anger, she went to bang on Brandon's door and confront him.

Brandon woke with a jolt, hearing a banging noise. For a moment, he was disorientated. Where was Angel? She'd fallen asleep in his arms last night. But the bed was empty and the bathroom door was wide open.

Then he realised that someone was still banging on his door. 'Coming, coming,' he mumbled, and grabbed a towel to cover himself.

When he opened the door, Angel stood there, looking ragingly angry. He frowned. 'Angel? What's the matter?'

'What's the matter? You know perfectly well what the matter is.' She thrust her phone at him. 'Look at this. Are you proud of yourself?'

His frown deepened as he saw the headline: *Racing Champ's Successful Takeover.*

'What? I don't understand.'

'Don't play cute with me—it says "sources at the company" told them that Stone's is taking over McKenzie's. They're not going to be stupid enough to print something like this without your agreement, because they know if it's not true they'll end up with a court ordering them to pay damages.' She dragged in a breath. 'And it talks about the Frost. In detail. You're the only one outside McKenzie's and Triffid who knew about it.' Her lip curled. 'You're a player, and I've been incredibly stupid.'

What? But he hadn't talked to the press. At all. He had no idea where this was coming from. 'Angel, I—'

'Save it. I don't want to hear any excuses. I'm making my own way home—and I don't want to see you again. Ever. But I suggest you contact your precious sources at the paper and get this story corrected, or you'll be hearing from my lawyers.' She lifted her chin. 'And if I can't talk Triffid out of dumping the Frost and McKenzie's, you'll be hearing from my lawyers anyway. Because doing something this underhand *has* to be against the law.'

'Angel—' he tried again.

'Goodbye, Brandon,' she said, and walked off.

He grabbed some clothes, but by the time he'd pulled

them on she was nowhere to be seen. It was pointless trying to follow her.

He dragged a hand through his hair and tried to focus. What did he do now?

First things first, he needed to look at the news report properly so he knew exactly what he was working with. And as he worked his way through it, he groaned. She was right. It did claim that the source was someone at Stone's—and she was also right that the paper wouldn't have printed that if it wasn't true. The media had to be careful about defamation law.

But how the hell had the press got the information about the Frost? He hadn't said a thing to anyone except Angel herself.

He pushed away the fact how hurt he was that she thought he could do something like this to her. The emotional stuff could come later. First, he needed to fix this.

Who at Stone's would break a story like this? Who had leaked the news about the Frost?

He had one nasty thought about the person at Stone's—but no, surely…

There was only one way to find out. He rang the newspaper. After being put through to four different people, eventually he got the answer he'd been dreading. Which left him no choice but to act.

And this wasn't something he could do by phone.

He desperately wanted to see Angel and sort things out between them, but he needed to fix things before he talked to her. He showered swiftly, changed, checked out of the hotel without bothering with breakfast and drove back to Oxford.

Finally, he pulled up outside his uncle's house and rang the doorbell.

'Oh. You,' Eric said when he opened the door, not even looking surprised to see Brandon.

'Yes, me. We need to sit down and talk.'

Eric scoffed. 'You're not even going to thank me for doing your job for you?'

'Doing my...?' Brandon looked at him in disbelief. 'You didn't do my job, Eric. What you did was to cause a huge amount of trouble. It was unprofessional, underhand and unacceptable. That's not how we do things at Stone's.'

'Rubbish. You were dragging your feet about the take-over. We all knew what the outcome was going to be, but you weren't man enough to seal the deal. So someone had to give her a push.'

'You didn't give her a push. She wasn't selling.' Much as Brandon wanted to shake his uncle until his teeth rattled, violence wouldn't make anything better. 'How did you get the information about the Frost?'

Eric shrugged. 'If you will leave your PC on with your mail program up, you can expect people to read it.'

Brandon stared at him, hardly able to believe what he was hearing. 'What? You went into my office and snooped?'

'It's something that affected Stone's, and I'm on the management team. I had a right to know.'

So that was what this was about. Brandon gritted his teeth. 'Eric, I know you're angry that I'm in charge, but this has to stop. Now. I don't want you in the factory any more.'

'Are you trying to sack me? You can't,' Eric sneered.

'Actually, as the CEO of Stone's, I could sack you for gross misconduct,' Brandon said. 'I've put up with you sniping at me for years, because you're my uncle and I've been trying to cut you some slack, but this isn't healthy for anyone, And, by telling the press we're going to take over McKenzie's when we're not doing anything of the kind, you've damaged both our companies. She could sue us for misrepresentation—and more, if her business goes under.'

Eric flapped a dismissive hand. 'She's a McKenzie, so who cares if her business goes under?'

'*I* care,' Brandon said.

'Because you've got the hots for her.'

'I'm not discussing my private life. I'm discussing the business.' He raked a hand through his hair. 'Eric, you need to retire.'

'Jump before I'm pushed, you mean?'

'You're not happy in the company.'

'Are you surprised, with you walking in and taking the place I should've had?' he snarled.

'But,' Brandon said, 'I'm making a success of it. If I was making a total mess of things, then you'd have every right to be fed up with me. But I'm not making a mess of things. I've got a vision for our company. And you're working against me rather than with me. It's not helping either of us.'

'But I've worked there all my life.'

'Maybe,' Brandon said, 'it's time for you to find out what actually makes you happy. Even before I took over from Dad, you weren't happy.'

Eric said nothing.

'I don't want to sack you. But surely you can see this isn't working.'

'So you want me to jump before I'm pushed,' Eric said again.

Brandon sighed. 'Eric, I need my team to work with me. You're clearly not prepared to do that. What other option do I have?'

'Let me take over—as I should've done when your father retired,' Eric said, his face suffused with anger and resentment.

'I'm a second son, too,' Brandon said softly. 'If Sam hadn't been killed—'

'If Sam hadn't been forced to race because you'd just had to show off on the ski slopes and broke a rib,' Eric cut in.

'I have to live with that every single day,' Brandon said. 'But, as I was trying to say, if Sam hadn't been killed, I would've been happy to work with him here in whatever capacity he wanted me. Or I might've chosen to go and set up my own business, find my own way. Maybe it would've made you happier if you'd done that.'

Eric said nothing,

'Why do you hate the McKenzies so much?' That was the thing Brandon really couldn't understand.

'Because of Esther,' Eric said, 'and Angel McKenzie is the spit of her grandmother.'

Brandon sighed. 'Two men fell in love with the same woman. She chose one of them. It was seventy years ago. Don't you think it's way past time we moved on from that?'

'Barnaby was my father,' Eric said, 'and I spent my childhood seeing how miserable my mother was because she never matched up to Esther in his eyes. It was why she used to drink. Why she died when I was five.'

Brandon knew his grandmother had died young, but he hadn't realised she'd had a drinking problem that had led to her death. 'That's really sad for both of them,' he said, 'and I'm sorry I never actually knew my grandmother. But don't you think it's Granddad's fault rather than Esther's that Alice drank? Plus my father's five years older than you and he saw it all, too, but he's not bitter towards the McKenzies.' Or was he? Was that why he'd tried to buy McKenzie's in the last recession?

'You'll never understand,' Eric said.

'No, because thankfully my parents were happy to-

gether.' Though Brandon could understand now why Eric
had never married, with his parents as such an unhappy
example. Brandon's father, being slightly older, had maybe
seen happier times that had prompted him to get married,
but he'd also obviously decided that he didn't want his
son's childhood to be as miserable as his own had been.
Even though Larry had followed in his father's footsteps
as a ruthless workaholic.

'I'm sorry you suffered, Eric, and I'm sorry my grandmother suffered, but it doesn't excuse what you've done
to Angel McKenzie. She worked really hard on designing
a car that was going to be used in a movie—the car that
would make everything all right again at McKenzie's. The
car's amazing.'

'So you've actually seen it?'

'Yes. She trusted me enough to let me see the prototype. I let her down because I was stupid enough to think
that nobody at Stone's would go and snoop on my computer and then use private emails against someone who's
totally blameless. And I hate to think that this family feud
is going to fester and ruin things for this generation, too.'

'But they're McK—'

'They're *people*. Like you and me,' Brandon cut in. 'I
understand now why you did what you did, but it's *wrong*,
Eric. And hurting other people isn't going to change what
happened in the past.'

'Nothing's going to change the past.'

'I know. But we can learn from the past and change the
future,' Brandon said. 'Which is what I'm going to try to
do. And I'd like you to do the right thing and retire right
this very second—and get some counselling, which I will
pay for personally.'

Eric lifted his chin. 'And if I don't?'

'Then,' Brandon said, 'I'll sack you for gross misconduct. And I'll face up to all the consequences of that, though I'm pretty sure Dad will agree with me. But whether you retire or I have to sack you, I want you to get counselling. You can't keep living with this kind of misery, Eric, and you can't keep making other people's life hell just because you're miserable. It doesn't help you and it doesn't help anyone else.'

'I...' The fight suddenly went out of Eric and his shoulders slumped. 'So you're taking a McKenzie's side against me. So much for blood being thicker than water.'

Brandon's patience was close to snapping, but he thought of Angel. How would she deal with this? Kindly, he'd guess. 'I'm trying to do the right thing,' Brandon said. 'And I really have to ring LA now and grovel my head off to see if I can fix this for Angel and persuade the film company not to cancel the contract. Because she really, really doesn't deserve what you did to her.'

'But I've got stuff at the factory.'

'Then I'll pack it up for you and bring it to you.'

'Scared I'm going to do something like burn the factory down?' Eric sneered.

'I sincerely hope you wouldn't,' Brandon said. 'But, actually, I'm trying to spare you any embarrassment or pain.'

'Bossing me around, like the jumped-up little—'

'Eric, this isn't good for you,' Brandon cut in. 'You need to let it go. And you need help.'

'I don't need anything from you.'

'If that's what you think, fine, but I need something from you before I go. Your keys to the factory.' He held his hand out.

'But—'

'You don't work there any more—you've retired,' Brandon said.

Eric suddenly crumpled. 'What am I going to do with my life now?'

'Make it happier,' Brandon said softly.

Finally, Eric handed over the keys. He looked as if he'd aged two decades in as many minutes. It made Brandon feel guilty, but he knew he was doing the right thing. Something he probably should've done years ago.

'Thank you,' Brandon said. Once he was back in his car, he called his father and filled him in on what had just happened. 'I don't think Eric should be alone right now,' he finished.

'I'll come over and see him. You did the right thing,' Larry Stone said. 'I'm sorry you had to deal with this, Bran. I should've done more when we were kids or realised how unhappy he was.'

'Dad, you were a kid yourself.' He paused. 'Would you have a problem with me seeing Angel McKenzie? After the way your dad was with your mum, I mean?'

'Because of Esther?' Larry paused. 'If you'd asked me that a few years ago, I might've said yes. But losing Sammy taught me a hard lesson. Love's always more important than business. So if that's how you feel about her, follow your heart. Go after her. Don't let business get in the way.'

'Thanks, Dad. I'm glad we're not going to have to do a Romeo and Juliet.' Brandon took a deep breath. 'You'll like her. She's bright and she's sweet. And her designs are amazing.'

'Gina likes her. That's good enough for your mother. And what's good enough for your mother is good enough for me,' Larry said. 'So what are you going to do?'

'Hope that I can fix things—and then that she'll talk to me.'

'Good luck. And we're behind you all the way,' Larry

said. 'I know you've got this, but call me if you need anything.'

'Thanks, Dad.' Brandon appreciated the support.

His next call was to Triffid's legal team. 'My name's Brandon Stone, and we need to talk,' he said.

'We're not looking to do business with you, Mr Stone,' the lawyer said.

'No, but you've been dealing with McKenzie's and you're under the misapprehension that my company's taking hers over. We're not. And Angel had nothing to do with any of those leaks about the Frost. I'm getting a correction printed in the news.'

'What does that have to do with us?' the lawyer asked.

'That car's amazing. It'll be perfect for your film. And you'd be shooting yourself in the foot if you tried to get someone else to design you a car even half as good. Angel McKenzie is the best designer I've ever met, and she's got guts and integrity.'

'That's as may be, Mr Stone.'

'Think of the time and cost implications,' Brandon said. The bottom line was usually the one that worked in business. 'Your PR team could spin this so everyone wins. And I have some ideas that might interest you.'

'Go on,' the lawyer said.

It took another half hour, but finally the lawyer agreed to talk to his people and reinstate the contract.

Which left Brandon one last thing: to face Angel and persuade her to listen to him.

He tried ringing her, but he wasn't surprised that she refused to pick up. He left her a message: 'Angel, we need to talk. I understand why you're angry with me but things really aren't what they seem. I'm coming to find you so we can talk—and I'm not taking no for an answer.'

Where was she likely to be?

His guess was that she'd be at the factory, looking through her books and trying to work out where she could go next—which was just what he'd be doing in her shoes.

Grimly, he headed for the motorway. If he'd got it wrong and she wasn't at the factory, then he'd drive to her house and sit on her doorstep until she came home; and if that meant staying there all night then he'd do it.

Because he wanted a future with Angel.

The only thing that might work was if he opened his heart and told her everything.

And he'd just have to hope that she'd listen.

CHAPTER ELEVEN

WHEN BRANDON PULLED up at the factory, he could see Angel's Luna in the car park. So she was here: now all he had to do was persuade her to talk to him.

He pressed the intercom switch at the barrier to the car park.

'Hello?' a voice crackled.

'Hello—is that Security?' he asked.

'Yes.'

'Great. I've got a meeting with Ms McKenzie. Can you lift the barrier and let me in, please?'

'I'm afraid Ms McKenzie isn't here, Mr Stone.'

Uh-oh. He'd been careful not to mention his name, but Angel's security team knew who he was. So obviously she'd given them a description of him or his car, and told them not to let him in. He sighed. 'I appreciate your loyalty to her. But this is important.'

'I can't let you in, Mr Stone.'

'Have you ever really, really messed up?' he asked. 'Because I have. And I really want to make it right for her.'

The security guy said nothing.

'Please. I'm not going to cause a scene, I promise. I just want to apologise and ask her to let me explain. If she tells me to go, then I'll go without making a fuss,' Brandon said.

'I can't do that, Mr Stone.'

Brandon knew he was going to have to go for broke. 'If you realised that someone was the love of your life, and you only had one chance to tell them or you'd lose them for ever...'

There was silence, and he knew he'd blown it.

'OK. Thanks anyway,' he said. 'I'll have to resort to sitting on her doorstep until she talks to me. Even if it takes me a week.'

'If she tells you to go,' the security guard said, surprising him, 'then you go immediately.'

'Immediately,' Brandon agreed, relief flooding through him. 'Thank you.'

Angel was in her office, looking through some files on her desk, when he rapped on the door.

She looked up. 'I expressly told my security team not to let you in.'

'Don't blame them. It's my fault.'

'What do you want?'

'To talk to you.'

Her lip curled. 'I don't want to talk to you.'

'Angel. Please. Just give me five minutes, and if you still want me to leave after that, I'll go without a fuss.'

'Why should I even give you that?' she asked.

'Because you were right, and I owe it to you to grovel properly. Plus, if I go, you won't ever know the truth.'

She paused for so long he thought she was going to refuse. But then she nodded. 'All right. You've got five minutes.'

'The most important thing you need to know is that I've spoken to Triffid. They know the truth, and your contract's back on.'

'Supposing I don't want to work with them now?'

'That's your decision,' he said. 'But at least they know now the story wasn't true.'

'Why did you lie about it in the first place?'

'I didn't,' he said. 'I know the evidence all looks as if it points to me being the leak, so in your shoes I'd be livid with me too, but it wasn't me. The paper was quite specific: they spoke to a source close to the company. Not the CEO.'

She still didn't look convinced, and he sighed inwardly. How could he make her understand the truth, but without dragging Eric into it?

'The person who talked to the press no longer works for me,' he said carefully. 'And because I'd got to know you and thought about the way you deal with things, I dealt with the situation slightly differently than I would have done if I hadn't met you. I wanted to be fair, not ruthless.' He paused. This was the really sticky bit. But they didn't have a hope in hell of a future if he wasn't completely honest with her now. 'But I did lie to you about something else.'

She frowned. 'What?'

'When I first met you,' he said. 'I tried to play you.'

She went white. 'So you never wanted to date me in the first place. It was all to get me to sell to you.'

'When I met you,' he said, 'I'd lost my way. I felt responsible for Sam's death, and I didn't feel I deserved love. So, yes, I was cynical about it. I was cynical about everything. I dated you as a way to get close to you and charm you into selling the company to me.'

'I think you've said enough,' she said. 'Get out.'

'I haven't had my five minutes.'

'You don't need it.'

'Oh, but I do,' he said. 'Because that was just the starting point, and I've moved further than I ever thought possible. You've changed me, Angel. All the while I thought I was charming you, actually you were the one who charmed me.'

'Me? Her face was filled with disbelief. 'But I don't play with people like that.'

'I know. It's just how you made me feel. I'm a different person when I'm with you. I like who I am when I'm with you. And all the time I kept telling myself I wasn't falling in love with you and I'd get everything under control, I was in total denial. Because I fell in love with you, Angel. You helped me find my way back. You helped me see that Sam's death was an accident—yes, it was my fault that he was racing, but it wasn't my fault that the accident happened.' He paused. 'And Cumbria. When you and I—'

She went bright red. 'Do you have to bring that up?'

'Yes. Because you gave me something really, really precious.'

'My virginity?' She flapped a dismissive hand. 'It's just an embarrassment in today's world.'

'No. It meant something to you. And it means something to me, too. It means you trusted me.'

'While you were lying to me all along.'

'I,' he said, 'am a first-class idiot. I don't know how to make things right between us. I need your help—I need you to show me the way.'

'There isn't a way.'

'You once told me that there's always a way.'

'Not this time.'

He sighed. 'OK. I can't fix it between us, but I can fix the damage done to your company.' He paused. 'If you change your mind about working with Triffid, you've still got financial problems. I've seen your books. So here's my proposal: if you don't go with Triffid, I'll give you the backing you need.'

She shook her head, looking disgusted. 'So you're still trying to buy McKenzie's?'

'No. I'm offering you an interest-free loan,' he said. 'Not from Stone's but from me personally.'

'Why would you do that?'

'Because the Frost is an incredible car that deserves to be out there in the market, and I believe in you.'

Brandon believed in her.

Or so he said.

He'd already lied to her. Multiple times. How did she know he wasn't lying now?

Her suspicion must have shown on her face, because he said, 'There aren't any strings. I'd also like to marry you, but that's a separate issue. Whatever happens between you and me, I'm still backing your business, because I love you and I believe in what you're doing. I don't want McKenzie's to go under. You rescued me from my private hell. Now it's my turn to rescue you.'

She couldn't get her head round this. Someone at his company had done their best to destroy hers—and he was trying to tell her he *loved* her and wanted to marry her?

More like he'd seen her in the same way as her fellow students had seen her at college: a challenge to be conquered. She'd been so flattered that she'd let him charm her into bed. Worse still, she'd instigated it. How he must have laughed at her. Hadn't he just told her that it had been his original plan to charm her into selling McKenzie's to him? Her virginity had been a cushy little bonus.

And now he was trying to make her believe that he loved her.

Of course he didn't.

She'd just been a means to an end. Only she wasn't selling.

'You've had your five minutes,' she said. 'Please go.'

'I'm sorry you've ended up hurt because of something

that Stone's did,' he said. 'Hurting you is the last thing I wanted to do. And I don't know how to make it better. All I know is that I love you, and I don't want our family history getting in the way.'

'It isn't our family history. You *lied* to me, Brandon. You used me.'

He raked a hand through his hair. 'And I apologise for that. I've been lying to myself, too. But I swear I would never intentionally do anything to hurt you. I love you, Angel. I respect you. You know your business inside out, you're a first-class manager and you've kept McKenzie's going for much longer than anyone else I know could've done in your position. You're an amazing designer whose ideas really inspire me. And more importantly you're an amazing woman. The woman I want to spend the rest of my life with.' He dragged in a breath. 'Except I don't know how to convince you that I mean it. How to get your trust back.'

She didn't know how he could convince her, either.

As if her agreement with him showed in her face, he sighed. 'OK. I've had my five minutes. I don't have any flashy gestures or flashy words or flashy *anything* left. I could go and buy the biggest diamond in the world and offer it to you on one bended knee, but it wouldn't even begin to tell you how I feel about you. All I can do is tell you that I love you and I want to fix it. But I can't do it on my own. I need you to meet me halfway, to show me how to bridge this gap between us.'

Angel wasn't sure she knew how to bridge the gap, either. How could she learn to rebuild her trust in him, when he'd admitted that he'd lied right from the start?

'I've done the best I can to fix things. But please think about what I said. And if you want to talk—well, you know where you can find me.' His grey eyes filled with sadness, and he turned on his heel and left.

Angel wasn't sure how long she sat there just staring at the empty doorway and wondering how her life had turned so upside down, but then her video call buzzed.

Triffid's legal team.

She thought about ignoring it; but then again maybe she could salvage something for McKenzie's from the call. Her personal life might be in shreds, but that was no excuse for letting her staff down. With a sigh, she accepted the call.

'Miss McKenzie, I'm glad I caught you. I've been talking to our people since Mr Stone called me this morning, and…'

So Brandon hadn't lied about that. He really had called LA to tell them the story about the merger wasn't true.

'Sorry. Can you run that by me again?' she asked, when it became obvious that the lawyer was waiting for an answer and she'd missed most of what he'd said to her.

When she'd finished the call, she leaned back against her seat. Brandon hadn't just corrected the story, he'd come up with a host of ideas to spin it in McKenzie's favour. He wouldn't have done that if he'd been the person trying to bring McKenzie's down with rumours.

So maybe he'd been telling her the truth.

He'd said some things that had really hurt her. Things that had shown him in a horrible light. But he'd also said that she'd changed him and changed the way he saw things.

Now she'd thought about it, he'd changed her, too. From a quiet, nerdy engineer who was happiest in her overalls and with no social skills into a woman who wore a red dress and danced at a glittering ball. He'd given her confidence in herself.

And maybe he did love her. He'd let her drive the Mermaid; he'd stepped in when her hearing let her down, but without making her feel useless or stupid; he'd thought about her and what she'd like to do on their dates.

Brandon Stone was a decent, thoughtful, caring man who also just happened to be one of the most gorgeous men she'd ever seen. He made her heart beat faster, but it wasn't just because of the way he looked. It was because she liked being with him. She liked who she was when she was with him.

If you want to talk—well, you know where you can find me.

She did indeed.

She locked up the factory, stopped by her security team to thank them, and headed for Oxford.

Brandon was right where she expected to find him: in his aircraft hangar of a garage, dressed in scruffy overalls, polishing chrome on the Mermaid.

'You missed a bit,' she said, pointing to a tiny area on the rear bumper.

'Engineers. So picky,' he said.

'Yeah. We expect the best.'

'Which is no less than you deserve.'

She knew she was going to have to be the one to broach the issue—because she was the one who'd refused to discuss it before. 'I've been thinking.'

'Uh-huh,' he said, as if he was trying really hard to sound careful and neutral and not scare her away.

'Triffid called me. What you did—you didn't have to.'

'I rather think I did,' he said. 'It was Stone's fault that McKenzie's was damaged.'

'Temporarily.'

'My company. My responsibility to fix the damage.'

'But not,' she said, 'your *fault*. That's the second thing you've taken the blame for. Don't let there be a third.'

'Too late. I hurt you. And you can't deny that's my fault, Angel.'

'True,' she said, 'but you were also being honest. If I'd found out in six months' time that you'd only starting dating me to get your hands on McKenzie's, it would've hurt me a lot more. I'm glad you told me now, because it means we're starting with a clean slate. With the truth.'

His eyes brightened with hope. 'So does this mean I get a second chance?'

'There's been bad blood between our families for too long,' she said. 'I know my dad wrote your dad a letter when Sam was killed, but maybe your dad was too upset to reply.'

'I don't think he got the letter. Eric was helping to deal with all the corr—' Brandon stopped and grimaced. 'Eric again.'

'Eric *again*?' she queried.

'I'm guessing he threw the letter away.'

'I gathered that,' she said gently. 'But what I didn't get was the "again" bit—do you mean Eric was the one who talked to the press about the buyout and the Frost?'

'He thought I wasn't doing a good enough job at making you sell McKenzie's to me, so he put the pressure on. He knows now he did the wrong thing.' Brandon sighed. 'And it didn't help that he was so bitter about the past.' He filled her in on what Eric had told him about the family history.

'That's really sad,' Angel said. 'I'm sorry he had to go through that. Though it's not been a total bed of roses for my family either; my dad's older sister died from scarlet fever when he was five, and I'm an IVF baby.'

'I'm sorry, too. I didn't know all of that,' Brandon said.

'Why would you? I'm guessing maybe one or the other wanted to try to mend things at different points along the way, but they were all too stubborn. Maybe your grandmother wanted to come to my aunt's funeral, but thought it would be rubbing it in because she still had two children and Esther and Jimmy didn't. Or maybe she was afraid that if Barnaby tried to comfort Esther, it might end up…' She grimaced. 'Just as I'm guessing that Esther felt bad when Alice died, but maybe she and Jimmy didn't want to hurt Barnaby by rubbing their own happy marriage in his face.'

'They all wasted so much time,' Brandon said.

She sighed. 'The way I see it, life's so short. You just have to muddle through things together.'

'I agree.'

'So what did you do? You said that the person who talked to the press doesn't work for you any more. Don't tell me you sacked your uncle?'

'No. I asked him to retire—though I didn't actually give him a choice,' Brandon admitted.

'Maybe he could—'

'Be redeemed?' He nodded. 'That's why I'm making him have counselling, and I'm taking him to the counsellor myself. He needs to find what he really loves in life. And only then will he be able to be happy.'

'I hope so,' she said.

Brandon looked at her. 'I've found what I really love in life. You. And I admit I had underhand motives when I first met you, but I fell in love with you along the way. Cumbria was real.'

'I know.' She took a deep breath. 'But our families hate each other. My grandfather married the woman your grandfather loved, your dad tried to buy mine out, and…'

'I spoke to my dad,' Brandon said. 'He said that losing Sammy taught him that love's more important than business. He told me if I loved you, to go after you.'

'I spoke to my dad,' Angel said. 'He says if you hurt me, you have him to deal with.'

Brandon grinned. 'Which is exactly what I'd say to our daughter's boyfriend. That's what dads are supposed to do, be all gruff and protective.'

'Maybe we made a tactical error and should've talked to our mums, and got them to talk our dads round,' Angel said.

'Or we face them together and tell them the family feud ends now. They can judge us on our terms. Which is at face value,' Brandon said.

'You know, seventy-odd years ago, we started as the same company. Maybe that's how we should end the feud.'

He blinked, looking surprised. 'Are you offering to sell to me?'

'No. I was thinking more along the lines of a merger,' she said.

'Professional or personal?' he asked.

She spread her hands. 'Do you have a preference?'

'I'm greedy. I'll go for both,' he said. 'I love you, Angel. And I'm sorry things went bad.'

'Me, too. I didn't want to believe you'd betray me like that.'

'Pretty much any jury in the land would've convicted me on that evidence,' he said wryly. 'Including me. I don't blame you.'

'You said I made you see things differently. You make me see things differently, too,' she said. 'I like who I am when I'm with you.'

He coughed. 'You're missing three words, you know. I've said it to you at least three times.'

'True.'

He groaned. 'Do you want me to beg?'

'Depends.' Her heart did a tiny little flip. 'Would that be on one knee?'

'You engineers drive a hard bargain.' He fished a key

ring from his pocket and removed the key. 'Are you quite sure you don't want this to happen in some flashy restaurant overlooking the sea at sunset, with us both dressed up to the nines and vintage champagne on ice?'

'How can that possibly compare with this—the things we both love?' she said, gesturing to the classic cars around them. 'And I don't need vintage champagne. That mug of tea on your workbench looks good enough to me.'

He grinned, and dropped to one knee. 'Angel McKenzie, I love you. I want to design cars with you and have babies with you and be a better man just because you're by my side. Will you marry me?'

'I love you, too, Brandon. And I want to design flashy high-end cars with you, and have babies with you, and be braver than I think I am because you're by my side. Yes,' she said, and he slid the Mermaid's key ring onto her finger.

'This is only temporary, you know,' he warned. 'You get to choose whatever you want as an engagement ring.'

She smiled. 'This would do me.'

'You can't have a key ring as an engagement ring, Angel.' He paused. 'Though you can have it as your engagement present.'

She laughed. 'The perfect present for an engineer—something useful. Thank you.'

'It comes with a key, though,' he said, and pressed the key to the Mermaid into her hand.

Her eyes widened as she realised what he meant. 'You're giving me the Mermaid?'

He shrugged. 'Looks like it.'

'Brandon, you can't—'

He silenced her by standing up and kissing her. 'It's your grandfather's design. I spent months restoring it. And

I think my favourite person in the world should have my favourite car in the world—right along with my heart.'

'I… Thank you. I'm a bit overwhelmed. And I can't afford to give you anything nearly so expensive,' she said ruefully.

'I don't want a present,' he said softly. 'I just want you. Right by my side.'

'You've got it.'

He held her close. 'So we're agreed: it's a merger?'

'McKenzie-Stone,' she agreed.

'Maybe,' he said, 'we should double-barrel our names. *Both* of us.'

She stared at him in surprise. 'You'd change your name for me?'

'If it means I get to marry you, yes. And it'll show that our families are truly one.'

'I like that idea.' She kissed him. 'It's a deal.'

He kissed her back. 'The deal of a lifetime.'

EPILOGUE

'ALL SET?' ASKED Sadie McKenzie. 'Something old?'

'Esther's pearls,' Angel said.

'Something new's your wedding dress. Something borrowed?'

Angel lifted her left arm. 'Lesley lent me Alice's bracelet.'

'That leaves something blue.'

Angel grinned. 'Brandon sent me a package this morning.'

'Right.' Sadie paused. 'I'm going to ask you about this while Lesley's sorting out Jasmine's fairy wings and can't hear me. You're totally sure about this?'

'I am,' Angel said. 'More sure than I've ever been in my life.'

Sadie hugged her. 'He's lovely and he's crazy about you, and that's all that matters.'

'Mum, don't. You'll make me cry and Maria spent ages doing my make-up this morning.'

'I know, love. She's a sweetheart,' Sadie said. 'And I'm glad the rift between the Stones and McKenzies has finally been healed. I know your dad was a bit worried that it was all going to go wrong, but I think he and Larry have surprised themselves by actually liking each other.'

Brandon and Angel's doubts had vanished as soon as

their mothers had started talking. There was only one Stone who hadn't been welcoming. The one who also hadn't responded to the wedding invitation. Angel had talked Gina into giving her Eric's private mobile number and had called him, but when he hadn't picked up she'd left a message that she hoped would make him put aside his anger for one day and come to the wedding.

Between them, the mothers had taken over to organise the wedding. They'd agreed that it wouldn't be tactful for Brandon and Angel to marry in the Cambridge church where her parents and grandparents had been married; instead, they'd chosen a local stately home which had a small and very pretty fourteenth-century church on the estate. And the McKenzies and the Stones were all getting ready at the McKenzie family home.

There was a knock on the door. 'Can I come in?' Lesley Stone asked.

'Of course,' Angel called.

Lesley walked in. 'The bridesmaids and flower girls are all rea— Oh, my. You look beautiful,' she said to Angel.

Angel smiled. 'Thank you. And so do you. So Maria, Gina, Stephie and Jas are all done? We're done, too— aren't we, Mum?'

'Then I think it's time for the girls to have champagne,' Lesley declared, linking arms with both Sadie and Angel.

Downstairs, the bridesmaids, flower girl and matron of honour were waiting; all were wearing simple deep violet dresses with a sweetheart neckline and wide straps, slim-fitting and falling to their ankles. Jasmine was wearing fairy wings and a sparkly tiara, which made Angel smile even more. The perfect outfit for a perfect day.

'Look at you! Turn round, Angel,' Gina directed. 'Brandon isn't going to know what's hit him.'

'You look like a princess,' Jasmine said, her grey eyes wide.

Her dress was ivory, strapless and with a sweetheart neckline. There was lace on the bodice, and then layers of organza falling to her ankles. Her shoes, for once, weren't flat but were strappy high heels to match the bridesmaids' dresses.

'That's because your mummy's very good with make-up,' Angel said.

'No, it's because you're beautiful,' Stephie said. 'Don't argue. You're not allowed to argue with pregnant women.'

'Aren't our girls all gorgeous?' Sadie said to Lesley.

'Aren't they just?' Lesley said. 'And I'm so glad our family's going to be one.'

There was just enough time for one glass of champagne, and the cars were ready to take them to the church.

'You look beautiful,' Max said outside the church. 'And best of all I know Brandon's going to be exactly the kind of husband I want for you—a man who really loves you.'

There was a lump in her throat a mile wide. 'Thanks, Dad. It means a lot, knowing we have your approval.'

'He's a good man. And his family's all right. I think we understand each other, now,' Max said. 'Ready?'

'Ready.'

Angel walked through the doors holding her father's arm. The church was all soaring arches, full of light, and the ancient box pews were crammed full of their family and friends. There were white and lilac and deep purple flowers everywhere and the organist was playing 'Here Comes the Sun'.

Brandon was standing at the top of the aisle next to his father, who was his best man. Larry looked round and saw her, then nudged Brandon and whispered something.

Brandon looked round and his eyes were so full of love; Angel could see him mouth, 'I love you.'

And then she was at the aisle by his side, plighting her troth, repeating the words after the vicar.

Finally, the vicar smiled. 'You may now kiss the bride.'

'About time,' Brandon said with a grin, and gently peeled back her veil before bending her back over his arm and kissing her soundly, to the applause of the congregation.

The signing of the register was a blur, but then they were walking back down the aisle, and the church bells were pealing as they came outside. Everyone was pelting them with white dried delphinium petals and cheering as they walked down the little path to the gate through the wall to the ancient hall next door.

The house itself was a beautiful eighteenth-century mansion with pale gold bricks and white sash windows, a porticoed entrance, a red-tiled roof with dormer windows jutting out, and wisteria on the walls. The photographer took photographs of family groupings by the car, next to the wisteria and on the steps, then finally went up to the parapet on the roof of the house and took photos of the whole group from above.

'The perfect day,' Brandon said.

'Absolutely,' Angel agreed, though she was aware that one person from his family was missing. The one person they hadn't seen at the church.

They lined up with both sets of parents to do the meet-and-greet. Angel was humbled to realise how many people there were to wish them well: family, old friends, staff from both their factories, and some of Brandon's old racing colleagues. Everyone hugged them soundly, all wishing them every happiness for the future.

'I don't think he's coming,' Brandon said softly.

'Trust me, he will,' Angel said. 'I left a message on his voicemail. He'll be here.'

And then, at the end of the line, there he was.

Angel greeted Eric with a hug.

'I'm sorry I didn't make the church,' Eric said. 'And I'm sorry about...'

'It's fine,' Angel said.

'I just wanted to wish you both well for the future.'

'I'm really glad you came,' she said. 'I meant what I said in that message.'

'That it wouldn't be the same without me? Even though I wrecked everything?' He looked shocked.

'It was fixable,' she said, 'and we all wanted you here. All of us. Because you're part of our family.' She paused. 'And you had a point. We're merging the businesses. And I meant what I said about coming back to the factory as a consultant. I've been looking through some of your paperwork and I really like your ideas about new fuels. We want you on our team to build the first McKenzie-Stone car in seventy years.'

Eric blinked away the tears in his eyes. 'If Esther was half the woman you are, I can quite see why my grandfather lost his head over her.' He turned to Brandon. 'Look after her.'

'I'd never make the mistake of wrapping my wife up in cotton wool,' Brandon said with a smile. 'But I'd lay down my life for her. So, yes, I'll look after her.'

'And the same goes for me,' she added.

'You'll be good for each other,' Eric said, and gave them both a hug.

And then he shocked everyone by hugging Angel's parents, who reacted by hugging him back.

'I have a feeling,' Brandon said, 'that everything's going

to be just fine. Come and sit down for our wedding breakfast, Mrs McKenzie-Stone.'

She smiled. 'I'd be delighted, Mr McKenzie-Stone.'

'To us,' he said softly at the table, lifting a glass. 'And our families. Joined at last.'

* * * * *

If you loved this book, don't miss
FALLING FOR THE SECRET MILLIONAIRE
by Kate Hardy.
Available now!

If you enjoyed this feel-good romance, watch out for
HER PREGNANCY BOMBSHELL
by Liz Fielding,
part of the SUMMER AT VILLA ROSA *miniseries.*

MILLS & BOON®
Hardback – May 2017

ROMANCE

The Sheikh's Bought Wife	Sharon Kendrick
The Innocent's Shameful Secret	Sara Craven
The Magnate's Tempestuous Marriage	Miranda Lee
The Forced Bride of Alazar	Kate Hewitt
Bound by the Sultan's Baby	Carol Marinelli
Blackmailed Down the Aisle	Louise Fuller
Di Marcello's Secret Son	Rachael Thomas
The Italian's Vengeful Seduction	Bella Frances
Conveniently Wed to the Greek	Kandy Shepherd
His Shy Cinderella	Kate Hardy
Falling for the Rebel Princess	Ellie Darkins
Claimed by the Wealthy Magnate	Nina Milne
Mummy, Nurse...Duchess?	Kate Hardy
Falling for the Foster Mum	Karin Baine
The Doctor and the Princess	Scarlet Wilson
Miracle for the Neurosurgeon	Lynne Marshall
English Rose for the Sicilian Doc	Annie Claydon
Engaged to the Doctor Sheikh	Meredith Webber
The Marriage Contract	Kat Cantrell
Triplets for the Texan	Janice Maynard

MILLS & BOON®
Large Print – May 2017

ROMANCE

A Deal for the Di Sione Ring	Jennifer Hayward
The Italian's Pregnant Virgin	Maisey Yates
A Dangerous Taste of Passion	Anne Mather
Bought to Carry His Heir	Jane Porter
Married for the Greek's Convenience	Michelle Smart
Bound by His Desert Diamond	Andie Brock
A Child Claimed by Gold	Rachael Thomas
Her New Year Baby Secret	Jessica Gilmore
Slow Dance with the Best Man	Sophie Pembroke
The Prince's Convenient Proposal	Barbara Hannay
The Tycoon's Reluctant Cinderella	Therese Beharrie

HISTORICAL

The Wedding Game	Christine Merrill
Secrets of the Marriage Bed	Ann Lethbridge
Compromising the Duke's Daughter	Mary Brendan
In Bed with the Viking Warrior	Harper St. George
Married to Her Enemy	Jenni Fletcher

MEDICAL

The Nurse's Christmas Gift	Tina Beckett
The Midwife's Pregnancy Miracle	Kate Hardy
Their First Family Christmas	Alison Roberts
The Nightshift Before Christmas	Annie O'Neil
It Started at Christmas...	Janice Lynn
Unwrapped by the Duke	Amy Ruttan

MILLS & BOON®
Hardback – June 2017

ROMANCE

Sold for the Greek's Heir	Lynne Graham
The Prince's Captive Virgin	Maisey Yates
The Secret Sanchez Heir	Cathy Williams
The Prince's Nine-Month Scandal	Caitlin Crews
Her Sinful Secret	Jane Porter
The Drakon Baby Bargain	Tara Pammi
Xenakis's Convenient Bride	Dani Collins
The Greek's Pleasurable Revenge	Andie Brock
Her Pregnancy Bombshell	Liz Fielding
Married for His Secret Heir	Jennifer Faye
Behind the Billionaire's Guarded Heart	Leah Ashton
A Marriage Worth Saving	Therese Beharrie
Healing the Sheikh's Heart	Annie O'Neil
A Life-Saving Reunion	Alison Roberts
The Surgeon's Cinderella	Susan Carlisle
Saved by Doctor Dreamy	Dianne Drake
Pregnant with the Boss's Baby	Sue MacKay
Reunited with His Runaway Doc	Lucy Clark
His Accidental Heir	Joanne Rock
A Texas-Sized Secret	Maureen Child

MILLS & BOON®
Large Print – June 2017

ROMANCE

The Last Di Sione Claims His Prize	Maisey Yates
Bought to Wear the Billionaire's Ring	Cathy Williams
The Desert King's Blackmailed Bride	Lynne Graham
Bride by Royal Decree	Caitlin Crews
The Consequence of His Vengeance	Jennie Lucas
The Sheikh's Secret Son	Maggie Cox
Acquired by Her Greek Boss	Chantelle Shaw
The Sheikh's Convenient Princess	Liz Fielding
The Unforgettable Spanish Tycoon	Christy McKellen
The Billionaire of Coral Bay	Nikki Logan
Her First-Date Honeymoon	Katrina Cudmore

HISTORICAL

The Harlot and the Sheikh	Marguerite Kaye
The Duke's Secret Heir	Sarah Mallory
Miss Bradshaw's Bought Betrothal	Virginia Heath
Sold to the Viking Warrior	Michelle Styles
A Marriage of Rogues	Margaret Moore

MEDICAL

White Christmas for the Single Mum	Susanne Hampton
A Royal Baby for Christmas	Scarlet Wilson
Playboy on Her Christmas List	Carol Marinelli
The Army Doc's Baby Bombshell	Sue MacKay
The Doctor's Sleigh Bell Proposal	Susan Carlisle
Christmas with the Single Dad	Louisa Heaton

MILLS & BOON®

Why shop at millsandboon.co.uk?

Each year, thousands of romance readers find their perfect read at millsandboon.co.uk. That's because we're passionate about bringing you the very best romantic fiction. Here are some of the advantages of shopping at www.millsandboon.co.uk:

* **Get new books first**—you'll be able to buy your favourite books one month before they hit the shops

* **Get exclusive discounts**—you'll also be able to buy our specially created monthly collections, with up to 50% off the RRP

* **Find your favourite authors**—latest news, interviews and new releases for all your favourite authors and series on our website, plus ideas for what to try next

* **Join in**—once you've bought your favourite books, don't forget to register with us to rate, review and join in the discussions

Visit **www.millsandboon.co.uk**
for all this and more today!